GORDON KORMAN

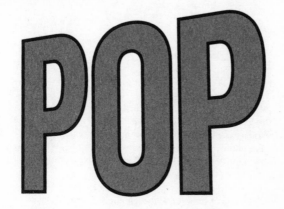

Balzer + Bray

An Imprint of HarperCollins*Publishers*

Balzer & Bray is an imprint of HarperCollins Publishers.

Pop

Copyright © 2009 by Gordon Korman

All rights reserved. Printed in the United States of America.

Library of Congress Cataloging-in-Publication Data

Korman, Gordon.

Pop / by Gordon Korman. — 1st ed.

p.   cm.

"HarperTeen."

Summary: Lonely after a midsummer move to a new town, high-school quarterback Marcus Jordan becomes friends with a retired professional linebacker whose erratic behavior confuses him, until Marcus discovers that the player is actually suffering from a neurological disease.

ISBN 978-0-06-174228-6 (trade bdg.) — ISBN 978-0-06-174230-9 (lib. bdg.)

[1. Football—Fiction.   2. Alzheimer's disease—Fiction.   3. High schools—Fiction.   4. Schools—Fiction.   5. Moving, Household—Fiction. 6. Divorce—Fiction.]   I. Title.

PZ7.K8369Pop 2009   2008052106

[Fic]—dc22   CIP
                                                                              AC

Typography by Carla Weise

09 10 11 12 13   CG/RRDB   10 9 8 7 6 5 4 3 2 1

❖

First Edition

In memory of my grandmother, Claire Silverman.
I remember what you couldn't.

CHAPTER ONE

Marcus Jordan killed the motor on his Vespa and surveyed the flowering shrubs and tall maples surrounding him. Nice. Picturesque, even.

More like *The Twilight Zone.*

For starters, the name—Three Alarm Park, after some chili cook-off that used to be held there in the sixties or something.

Marcus jumped down, pulling the gym bag off his shoulders. From it, he produced the items that would turn Three Alarm Park into a practice facility—a regulation football, a length of rope, and a round, plastic picture frame with the glass knocked out.

He looked around, noting that the only other living creature was a squirrel. This was the fourth straight day he'd trained here, and he'd yet to exchange a word of conversation with anybody but himself. Dead summer— great time to move to a new state. *Thanks, Mom.*

He tossed the rope over a high branch and strung up the picture-frame hoop. Then he started the target swinging gently and retreated about ten yards.

Hike!

Just like he'd done a million times before, he took three steps back and let fly.

The ball sizzled, a perfect spiral, missing the hoop by at least four feet.

Marcus snorted. Lonely *and* lousy. A one-two punch. With the added insult of having to chase down your own pass so you could mess it up all over again.

He worked his way up to four for ten, then eleven for twenty, and then he broke out the water bottle to give himself a party. Here in the middle of the open field, the only protection from the August sun was a large granite modern art statue titled *Remembrance*, which looked like a titanic paper airplane had fallen from the sky and buried its nose in the grass at a forty-five-degree angle. A river of perspiration streamed down the middle of Marcus's back. So he did what any self-respecting football player would do. He cranked it up a notch. Football was the only sport where adverse weather conditions made you go harder instead of quitting. He'd still be out here if it were only ten degrees and he were slogging through knee-deep snow and blizzard conditions.

Intermission—a dozen laps around the field, to *really* feel the pain. Then he was throwing again, from different angles and farther away. His completion percentage went down, but his determination never wavered. There was something about launching a football thirty-five or forty yards and having it go exactly where you aimed it. To a quarterback, it was as basic as breathing.

Sucking in a lungful of moist, heavy air, Marcus pumped once and unleashed the longest pass of the day, a loose spiral that nevertheless seemed to have a lot of power behind it. It sailed high over the apex of the Paper Airplane before beginning its downward trajectory toward the hoop.

For the first time in four days, Marcus spied another human being in the park. The figure was just a blur across his field of vision. It leaped into the air, picked off the pass, and kept on going.

The receiver made a wide U-turn and, grinning triumphantly, jogged up to Marcus.

Marcus smiled too. "Nice catch, bro—"

He was looking at a middle-aged man, probably around fifty years old. He was tall and built redwood solid. But the guy ran like a gazelle and had caught the ball with sure hands, tucking it in tight as he ran. He had definitely played this game before.

"Sorry," Marcus added, embarrassed.

"For what?" The man flipped him the ball. "Making you look bad?"

"I just thought—never mind. My name's Marcus. Marcus Jordan."

With lightning hands, the man knocked the ball loose, scooped it up on the bounce, and bellowed, "Go deep!"

Starved for company, Marcus did not have to be asked twice. He took off downfield, glancing over his shoulder.

"No—*deep!*"

"I'm running out of park!" Marcus shouted, but kept on going, his breath growing short. Another backward glance. The ball was on its way. Marcus broke into a full sprint. The old guy had an arm like a cannon!

He took to the air in a desperation dive. For an instant, the ball was right there on his fingertips. He had it. . . .

The ground swung up quickly and slammed him, and the pass bounced away. He lay there for a moment, hyperventilating and spitting out turf. The next thing he saw was the fifty-something-year-old, beaming and pulling him back to his feet.

"Way to miss everything."

"You overthrew me a little," Marcus said, defending himself.

The man plucked the ball off the grass. "You couldn't catch a cold, Mac."

"It's Marcus," he amended. "And you are . . . ?"

The old guy scowled. "Your worst nightmare if you don't quit pulling my chain."

Marcus flushed. "What should I call you?"

"Try Charlie, stupid. *Heads!*" He punted the ball straight up in the air.

The kick was very high, silhouetted against the cobalt blue sky, tiny and soaring.

Marcus was instantly on board, shuffling first one way and then the other as he tried to predict where it would come down. For some reason, it was very important to make this catch, especially since he'd screwed up the other one. It was his natural competitiveness, but there was something more. This Charlie character might be weird, but his enthusiasm had sucked Marcus in.

The ball plunged down, and Marcus gathered it into his arms.

Something hit him. The impact was so jarring, so unexpected, that there was barely time to register what was happening. It was Charlie—he'd rammed a rock-hard shoulder into Marcus's sternum and dropped him where he stood. The ball squirted loose, but Marcus wasn't even aware of it. He lay like a stone on the grass, ears roaring, trying to keep from throwing up his breakfast.

Gasping, he scrambled to his feet, squaring off against his companion. "What was that for?"

"I love the pop! Sometimes you actually hear it go *pop!*"

"That was the sound of my head coming off," Marcus muttered.

"Come on, you here to play or what?" Charlie tucked the ball under one arm and charged forward like a freight train, picking up speed.

Marcus was stunned. *He's crazy!* Followed by another thought: *He's an old man. What am I afraid of?*

Marcus held his ground, bouncing lightly on the balls of his feet, ready to strike. As a quarterback, he'd never had tackling at the top of his résumé, but he'd gone through the drills like everybody else. He focused on his opponent's hips, hesitating at the sheer size of the guy and the power and athleticism of his stride. This was going to hurt, probably more than a little. Swallowing his nervousness, he sprang, catching Charlie just above the knees.

Hard contact resonated up and down Marcus's body. The man was a strong runner with a surprisingly low center of gravity. In the end, though, physics was on Marcus's side. The textbook hit knocked Charlie's legs right out from under him.

As they crunched to the ground, Marcus's pain mingled with remorse. What if he'd hurt the man?

But Charlie was cackling with glee. "That's more like it!"

Relieved, Marcus grabbed the ball away and barked, "Now, *you* go deep!" It never crossed his mind that this "old man" wouldn't comply.

Charlie didn't disappoint. He was off and galloping. Not only was he going along with it, but he seemed to be running an elaborate pass pattern. He bumped an imaginary defender at five yards, then faked an out before breaking down the middle, running full bore.

Marcus got so involved in watching that he almost forgot to throw. But he did—a terrible pass that was sure to sail ten feet over Charlie's head.

"Sorry—" His breath caught in his throat as he realized that his companion wasn't stopping.

Adjusting his route, Charlie scampered right up one of the granite flukes on the *Remembrance* sculpture. Close to the top, he leaped, snatching the ball out of thin air as it sailed over the Paper Airplane. Marcus waited for the old guy to come crashing to the ground, twenty feet below. Instead, the toes of his sneakers somehow found the narrow ledge in the stone, and he landed, swaying as he struggled to maintain balance.

The cry of triumph was ripped from Marcus's throat before the event had even fully registered. It had to be the greatest individual effort he'd seen since taking up football. Quarterback and receiver celebrated like this was the winning touchdown in the Super Bowl.

Nor did Charlie feel any need to come down from his tenuous perch on the statue. He began a victory dance right where he was.

"I'm not calling the ambulance when you slip!" warned Marcus, laughing.

It only made the old guy show off even more. He was as sure-footed as a mountain goat, soft-shoeing as he waved to an imaginary crowd.

Time-tested football strategy held that when the

passing game is working, you launch an air war. They ran slants, curls, posts, and flags, making acrobatic catches and spectacular wipeouts. After a week of only his mother and his own thoughts for company, Marcus wasn't inclined to ask too many questions—like how come this middle-aged guy had nothing better to do than toss a ball around with a teenager.

"Over the middle!" Charlie commanded, waving Marcus into a crossing pattern about fifteen yards deep.

Charlie's muscular arm snapped forward. The pass was on its way, drilling through the air at bullet speed. Marcus reached for it, but he misjudged the angle. It sizzled between his hands, practically leaving a trail of smoke behind it. Frozen in their tracks, he and Charlie watched it leave the park.

Crash!

They didn't see it happen, but the sound was unmistakable. When they got to the fence, there sat the football: in the passenger seat of a Toyota Camry, clearly visible through the shattered side window.

"Great," groaned Marcus. This definitely wasn't the introduction to the community he'd had in mind. "I guess we have to leave a note and offer to pay—"

Nothing could have prepared him for his companion's reaction to the crisis. Charlie took one look at the broken car window, vaulted the gate, and pounded down the street at an astonishing rate of speed. He never looked back. In fifteen seconds, he was simply a retreating dot.

Of all the strange things about a very strange person, this one had to take the prize. Here was the teenager, ready to own up and make restitution. And here was the mature adult, fleeing the scene like an irresponsible kid.

CHAPTER TWO

RAIDERS LOOK TO REPEAT PERFECTION

What's better than perfect? Just ask quarterback Troy Popovich and the defending Hudson Valley champion Raiders of David Nathan Aldrich High School. The Little Team That Could finished with an 11–0 record and championship gold last season. Hard to top? Not for the boys from Kennesaw. With only four departing seniors, the Raiders think they can run the table again this year and carve themselves a place in Hudson Valley football history.

The quest for double perfection begins on August 18 with the opening of summer workouts. Good luck, Raiders!

Last week, when the movers had unloaded the truck, Marcus's first act of unpacking had been to tape that clipping to his mirror. It was the one consolation for pulling up roots in the only place he'd known in sixteen years of life and laying them down in a completely different part of the country—he'd be going to a school with a first-class football program.

Mom had made that article from the *Kennesaw Advocate* the keystone of her sales pitch. By that time, she'd already known that the *Advocate* would be her new employer. Of course, her job as staff photographer was just how Barbara Jordan paid the bills. She had little interest in the inevitable prizewinning turnips and golf-ball-sized hailstones that dominated local news in a small town. She was putting together a book on the megalithic boulders scattered across upstate New York by the receding glaciers of the Ice Age. That was the reason behind their move to Kennesaw in the first place—pictures of rocks. The fact that it put fifteen hundred miles between them and Comrade Stalin—well, that was just gravy. When your ex was a control freak, distance was a good thing.

The good comrade, Marcus's father, had responded to the divorce with his usual flexibility. No joint custody, no weekend visits—just a laundry list of all the material advantages Marcus would enjoy if he forgot he'd ever had a mother. The Vespa had been the primo goodie on an almost irresistible menu. Stalin had even tried to demand it back when Marcus had opted to stay with Mom. *Classy.*

The purr of the Vespa's engine had become a bittersweet sound. Bitter because of the bike's role in the family breakup, and sweet because—well, it *was* pretty sweet. A Vespa was technically a scooter, but it could *move*. Back in Olathe, Marcus had earned himself three speeding tickets. Now he was speeding again, far from Kansas, with his bulky equipment bag balanced on his shoulders, streaking through town to Aldrich High School.

The sight of players on the field threw him. He'd called the athletic office three times to confirm the eleven-o'clock start. Yet here it was, only ten thirty, and a workout was already in progress.

He ditched the Vespa in the parking lot and took off at a run, heavy pads bouncing against his shoulders. Students were scattered around the sidelines and on the bleachers. On the field, coaches and trainers were leading the players through stretches and calisthenics. Good news. He hadn't missed much.

He turned to the first spectator he saw, a girl in a tank top and jean shorts. "Tryouts?"

He might as well have been asking about the nuclear launch security codes. Her expression was completely blank.

Undaunted, Marcus pulled aside a tall kid in pads and a scrimmage shirt. "Where's the sign-up table?"

The kid looked him over. "Don't know what you're talking about, man," he said blandly, and jogged away.

Marcus stood by the entrance to the locker-room hut, frowning, when a brunette in a cheerleading outfit strode up to him, her pretty features hardened into an all-business expression.

"How long does it take to get a bag of footballs?" she demanded. In a single motion, she wrenched the duffel off his shoulder and unzipped. A sweat- and bleach-stained jockstrap tumbled out and fell at her feet.

She glared at Marcus. "Cute."

"I think you've got me confused with somebody else," Marcus told her. "I just came here to try out."

A freckle-faced player whose body seemed like an endless pair of shoulders turned around. "You sure you're in the right place, man?"

"Let me guess—you're just field-testing your Halloween costume, then?" Marcus returned, a little annoyed.

Another Raider stepped forward, his helmet under his arm—a classic all-American pose. It was obvious from the deference shown by the other students that this newcomer was Big Man on Campus. His scrimmage jersey bore the number seven, which, coupled with the respect he commanded, almost certainly designated him as the quarterback.

Self-consciously, Marcus plucked his cup off the turf and stuffed it back in the bag.

"Is that how you win friends and influence people?" the QB asked Marcus.

Marcus took a deep breath. "I don't want a fight. I'm just looking for the tryouts."

"You found them—sort of."

"Well, where do I sort of check in?"

"We went eleven and oh last season," Number Seven told him.

"I heard about that."

"We only lost four seniors, and we replaced them with backups who are just as strong."

"You're good," Marcus concluded.

"If you were us, would you be making changes?"

"That depends," Marcus said. "If you've got somebody better, why not?"

Number Seven's eyes flashed. "And that's supposed to be you?"

Marcus shrugged. "That's why you have tryouts. To pick the best."

"You're looking at him," Number Seven stated flatly.

"You'll have to forgive Troy," the cheerleader put in sarcastically. "He's overcome with his own magnificence."

Troy cast her a warning glare, and she smiled back sweetly. Marcus upgraded his first impression. Pretty was an understatement. She was a knockout.

With effort, he tore his eyes off her. "I'm not saying you're no good," he told Troy. "I'm just saying I should have a shot."

The endless shoulders got in Marcus's face. "Last

year's eleven-and-oh season was thanks to Troy! His old man—"

"Shut up, Kevin," Troy interrupted.

Kevin backed off, but he didn't back down. "We've got a chance at another perfect season! We're not risking that because of some newbie."

"What's going on here?" bawled a voice with the tone and timbre of a buzz saw. Coach Barker muscled into the group. "Football is played with hands, feet, and body. The only time your mouth is open is so you can stick your guard in!"

"Got a wannabe here, Coach," Troy said apologetically.

The coach was an ordinary-sized man with a massive head that made him resemble an Easter Island monument. It pivoted on his slender neck until his sharp gaze was focused on Marcus.

"What's your name, son?"

"Marcus Jordan. I just moved here a couple of weeks ago. I'll be a junior."

The coach sized him up. "What's your experience?"

"I QB'd junior varsity at my old school in Kansas. Set a county record for total yards."

"A *JV* record," Troy pointed out.

Marcus addressed the coach. "I know you have a tight-knit unit, and I'm not trying to mess that up. I just want a chance to show what I can do."

"I'm always looking for new talent," Barker agreed.

"Tell you what. We'll set a time for you to work out with the JV squad. If you're as good as you say, you'll play JV this season. Then, next year, it'll be wide-open for you after these guys graduate in June."

Marcus shook his head. "If I can hack it now, I shouldn't have to wait."

"It's a public school, Coach," the cheerleader noted.

Troy snorted. "Yeah, you've gotten to be such a football expert from shaking your butt!"

"You never complained," she shot right back.

"All right, fair enough," the coach decided. "Suit up, and we'll give you a spin."

"But Coach—"

Barker's face flamed red. "Doesn't anybody do what I say anymore? Get back on the field! I want to see wind sprints." He turned to the cheerleader. "Alyssa, show Marcus where he can change."

"With pleasure," she announced, directing a pointed grin at Troy. She took Marcus by the hand and led him into the low hut that housed the locker rooms.

Marcus looked down at the spectacle of her fingers intertwined with his. "Sounds like you and Troy know each other pretty well." An over-the-shoulder glance confirmed that the quarterback was doing more glowering than sprinting.

"We're kind of on again, off again," she admitted blithely. "And on again. And off again. You get the picture."

He did. "How about right now?"

"Right now I'm staying away from stuck-up quarterbacks who think they own the world." She cast him a look that threatened to melt the fillings in his teeth. "But I'm keeping an open mind."

She kicked loudly at a door marked HOME and yelled, "If it's hanging out, cover it up! I'm coming in!" She marched him into the deserted locker room.

Marcus tossed his bag on the bench and waited for Alyssa to leave so he could change. Instead, she made herself at home on the bench.

"I double as equipment manager. So if you've got any equipment you want me to manage . . . I'm *kidding*!" She laughed, seeing him blush. "A yokel like you is going to get eaten alive at DNA. What brings you to our little moonscape?"

Marcus shrugged his shoulder pads on over his T-shirt. "My mom's a photographer. This area's important to a book she's working on."

"And your dad?"

"Out of the picture." He studied the pockmarks on the concrete floor. "I have to take off my pants now."

"Buzz kill," she grumbled, heading for the door.

Marcus tried not to watch her go—and failed.

Don't get distracted, he admonished himself. He had his tryout, but it was obvious nobody wanted him here, not even the coach. If he didn't star in the next few minutes, he'd never see the inside of this locker room again.

Outside the hut, he found Alyssa waiting for him. Troy was with her, and the two were in the middle of a whispered argument.

"I could jump his bones in the parking lot and you'd have nothing to say about it!" she was hissing. "You broke up with me, remember?"

Troy noticed Marcus at last. "Come on, hotshot. They're ready for you."

Coach Barker started with Marcus throwing to receivers running basic patterns across the field. Tight end Luke Derrigan failed to reach out to gather in a pass that came down eighteen inches in front of him. Calvin Applegate had to slow his post pattern to nearly a walk so he could avoid the next one falling into his arms. Ron Rorschach, the halfback, was actually struck in the chest letter high while his arms dangled at his sides.

"Guess it's not your day," Troy commented with false sympathy.

Marcus swallowed a sarcastic retort. The last thing he wanted was for the coach to see him trashing his own receivers, but it was pretty obvious what was going on here. Not a single pass was going to be completed today, and it was going to be the quarterback's fault.

Barker looked on contemplatively. "The attack of butterfingers seems to be contagious."

"It's easy to get stale in the off-season," Marcus offered lamely.

"You're not stale," the coach observed.

"I've been working out on my own," Marcus replied. "And with—a friend," he added with a strange smile, remembering Charlie at Three Alarm Park. The smile disappeared abruptly. What kind of grown man was so cheap that he would stiff a teenager rather than pay his share of one little broken window? Now Marcus would be stuck with the whole tab. The damaged Camry was no longer parked in the same spot, and its owner had not yet responded to Marcus's note. But he would, of course. And then Marcus would be out hundreds of dollars he didn't have.

The coach raked his players with a wave of hot lead. "We're going to do it again, and this time, consider it a tryout for all your jobs. Take a look at Jordan and tell me any of you are so good you can't be replaced." He stared down a protest from Troy. "Can it, Popovich. I know who calls the shots with these sheep. You think I'm blind *and* stupid?"

This time the exercise was very different, and the completion rate was one hundred percent. It was obvious that the quarterback wannabe had an accurate throwing arm.

Troy watched the whole thing, his complexion darkening with every catch. Marcus knew there was trouble coming when he saw Number Seven whispering from ear to ear along the informal formation lined up for the drill.

When he took the snap, the defensive line was upon

him in a full blitz. His own protection melted away like butter on a hot knife. Panicking, Marcus released the ball too soon. It was everything a pass shouldn't be—soft, sickly, and nowhere near the intended receiver.

The rushers veered off at the last second, never even touching him. He was left standing there, awkward, embarrassed, and thoroughly schooled.

Barker shook his head wanly. "When something looks too good to be true, it usually is."

Marcus was devastated. Had he blown his chance?

The coach's bobblehead swiveled toward Alyssa. "Can you get Marcus a playbook and a practice schedule?"

"I'll hook him up," she promised with a mischievous smile.

To Marcus, he said, "You're going to ride a lot of pine this season. We're deep, and we're a unit. I'm not going to jeopardize that, no matter how good you are."

"I'm just happy to be on board," Marcus assured him.

Alyssa ran to the scorer's table and returned with a thick manila envelope. "You have to sign for this. In blood."

He scribbled his signature and accepted the packet. "Are you security, too?"

"I've been known to get physical."

"Hey, Alyssa," called Troy. "The cheerleaders are practicing in the end zone."

"They'll wait for me," she replied serenely. "I'm

walking Marcus to his car."

She didn't try to bully her way inside the locker room while he was changing this time. He wasn't sure whether or not he was grateful.

When they reached the parking lot, the sight of the Vespa made her laugh out loud. "What's that, a Barney-Davidson?"

"It gets me where I'm going," he said defensively.

"You're making it really hard to be blown away by your manliness."

"What does Troy drive?" he challenged. "An M1 tank?" He climbed on and started the motor.

"Where you going?" she protested. "Aren't you going to offer me a ride?"

He shook his head. "Only one helmet."

She unzipped his duffel, pulled out his football headgear, and jammed it down over her lustrous brown hair.

As they tooled around the block, her warm breath tickling the side of his neck, Marcus was very much aware that her eyes never strayed from the football field where her on-again, off-again was practicing—and probably watching just as intently.

"Should I be insulted that you're only paying attention to me to stick it to him?" he asked.

She shrugged airily. "You can find gravity insulting. It won't help you levitate. Good workout, by the way."

"Yeah," he laughed. "Especially that water balloon I

heaved out on the last play."

He felt her shrug across his whole back. "It's not rocket science. When you're throwing at targets, you're Tom Brady. Put a blitzer in your face and you fold up like a lawn chair."

All the sexual tension of the moment evaporated like steam. In a single comment, she had completely articulated the sum total of his self-doubt as a football player. If even the head cheerleader could see that, he was in big trouble.

CHAPTER THREE

Gun-shy.

That had always been the knock on Marcus. He'd even read it about himself in the Olathe paper. He had all the right tools, the full range of weapons—and none of the guts. Comrade Stalin had been all over him about this. What was the point of playing high school football if it wasn't the direct road to NFL millions? Nothing was worth doing if it didn't lead to world domination.

The pass was a bullet, sizzling past the Paper Airplane and whistling dead center through the dangling picture frame. When it hit the ground forty yards away, it took out a divot. But Marcus drew no satisfaction from being able to throw such a perfect ball. He could launch one half a mile and have it swish through the eye of a needle, but it wouldn't do him any good if he fell to pieces every time a linebacker got close. All the practice in the world with picture frames wasn't going to change that—not unless the frames learned to hit back.

He was heading to retrieve the ball, dragging his feet, when a familiar tall figure hopped the hedge and jogged into Three Alarm Park.

A blizzard of thoughts swirled around Marcus's head: *He's a weirdo who doesn't have friends his own age. He broke a window and stuck me with the blame.* His internal voice was drowned out by Charlie's words from their last encounter: *I love the pop. . . .*

The old guy packed a wallop like a pile driver.

If I can take a hit from him, I can take one from anybody. . . .

He turned to the newcomer. "Tackle me."

If Marcus had been expecting the question "Why?"— it wasn't going to come. The man was up to full speed seemingly in the first step, a look of unholy glee on his middle-aged features. In a heartbeat, the gap between the two of them had vanished, and Charlie was airborne, his body parallel to the ground. Marcus didn't even try to get away—not that he could have if he'd wanted to. Powerful arms clamped around his midsection just as the tackler's shoulder struck, a battering-ram shot that knocked him both up and back. He hit the ground hard, but not half as hard as the impact when Charlie landed on top of him, a full-body hammer blow.

Dazed and grass stained, Marcus scrambled up, unable to imagine how so much pain in so many places could all come from a single collision. He struggled to assemble a string of curses, but the wind was so thoroughly knocked out of him that he mustered no more than a rasp. Without waiting for his breath to return, he launched himself at Charlie, hitting him low and sending him sprawling.

"Clip!" Charlie roared. "That's a ten-yard penalty!"

"No rules!" Marcus managed to wheeze.

The ball lay ignored a short distance away as the two traded tackles for the next forty-five minutes. Marcus knew he was taking the brunt of the exchange, but he was getting his licks in as well, never allowing himself more than a gasp or two before running back at his opponent.

How was it possible for a man of fifty plus to wipe up the park with a kid less than a third his age? And not just to do it, but to love doing it! Whenever Charlie was making bone-jarring contact, the expression on his face was nothing short of bliss. Like Mozart at the harpsichord or Edison tinkering with some invention—it was something he was just meant to do.

By the time they took a break, Marcus was one deep, penetrating ache from the top of his head to the tips of his toes. The only thing preventing him from limping was that both legs were equally bruised. He felt a distinct throb from each individual rib. Ditto his arms, his shoulders, and his back. If there was a spot on his entire body that wasn't in agony right now, he was too exhausted to find it.

He watched in amazement as Charlie scampered effortlessly up a steep groove in the Paper Airplane and relaxed in one of the granite folds. "You're a lightweight, Mac," he said disapprovingly. "You pack a pop like Tinker Bell."

"My name is Marcus." The misfire brought Marcus back to their previous meeting—more specifically, to how it had ended. "You know, you really stiffed me last week. The guy hasn't called yet, but that broken window is going to cost at least a couple hundred bucks."

"A lot of windows get broken around here," Charlie said airily. "Hard to keep them all straight."

Marcus bristled. "So that's how it's going to be. You throw the ball, and I pick up the tab for it?"

Charlie looked offended. "You know I'm good for it."

Marcus regarded the man stretched out on the sculpture. He was well dressed and groomed—definitely not a homeless person. This was the second time he'd appeared in the park in the middle of the afternoon, so he didn't seem to have a day job. But some people worked odd shifts, or nights. Teachers had summers off. If a sixteen-year-old kid could afford to pay for half the car window, there was no reason to believe a grown man couldn't pick up the other half. The question was, would he?

"Well, how do I get in touch with you when the guy

calls? Can I have your phone number?"

Charlie looked amazed. "You don't know it?"

"You never gave it to me. You took off the minute we heard the crash."

The man sat up, perching precariously on the angled granite. "Later. We'd better get some ice for your elbow or it's going to swell up like a balloon."

Lost in his extensive résumé of aches, Marcus hadn't really focused on the condition of his passing arm, which was turning black and blue. Now it consumed all his attention.

Luckily, Charlie knew exactly what to do. He led Marcus out of the park and up the street to the gas station on the corner. He stepped into the mini-mart, opened the freezer, and helped himself to a bag of ice. Then, in full view of the cashier, he blithely left without paying.

"Okay, let's see that arm."

Marcus waited for the clerk to follow and demand payment. Instead, the woman just chuckled and waved at the shoplifter.

"Friend of yours?" Marcus asked.

Charlie seemed distracted. "What?" He manipulated the bag, forming it into a compress for the injured elbow.

Marcus accepted it gratefully. "That feels good. I wish I could get my whole body in there." He sat down on a bus bench and turned to his companion, who was gone. He twisted around and found that Charlie was perched atop a seven-foot chain-link fence, looking like a bird on a wire.

"What is it with you?" Marcus blurted. "How come you can only relax in places where you can fall off and break your neck?"

Charlie grinned at him. "If you can't break your neck, it's not worth sitting there." But within thirty seconds, he was down again. "Gotta hop. See you tomorrow."

Marcus was taken aback. "Where? What time?"

"The usual," he called, loping down the street with easy, powerful strides that only pointed at the contrast with Marcus, who could barely move.

What "usual" was Charlie talking about? Both times they had met, it had been in Three Alarm Park, so that was probably the place. But the time?

Nothing was usual about Charlie.

Before returning to the park to reclaim his Vespa and gear, Marcus poked his head into the mini-mart. "I need to pay for the ice. My friend—uh—forgot."

The woman laughed. "He didn't forget. That's just Charlie. Don't worry about it. It'll get paid."

He remembered Charlie's words about the broken window: *You know I'm good for it.* Apparently, the mini-mart thought he was good for it too.

Who *was* this guy?

CHAPTER FOUR

Coach Barker's philosophy of keeping your mouth shut applied to players only. His own cavernous maw was in constant motion, and he seemed to have words of wisdom for every occasion, both on the field and inside the locker room.

"In football, your head is either in the game or up your butt!"

"If you think you're too good to block, you're not good enough to put on this uniform!"

"Only God knows more than the coach, and He's not the one wearing the whistle!"

"Your mommy can't help you on this field; your

only family is your team!"

If the last one was true, Marcus was definitely the black sheep of the clan. His teammates looked right through him, and spoke to him hardly at all. He was a part of the drills only when Barker directly ordered it. And after the whistle, when the players were hauling one another upright, Marcus was left on the grass like a discarded tackling dummy. They took their lead from Troy. To Number Seven, Marcus was an escapee from a leper colony.

Of all the Raiders, Ron Rorschach was the most sympathetic, but even he was unwilling to cross his quarterback. "You've got to see it from Troy's perspective. You're a big threat to him."

"A threat?" Marcus repeated bitterly. "Troy's like God in this place. If Coach tried to bench him, he'd be lynched!"

Ron shook his head. "Not a *football* threat."

Marcus followed Ron's gaze to the sidelines, where Alyssa was practicing with the cheerleaders. There was something about the way the uniform hung on her. It was exactly the same as what the other girls wore, yet it *wasn't*—almost as if sheer attitude could fill out a sweater and miniskirt. Spying Marcus, she winked and waved.

Marcus turned back to Ron. "Alyssa said they broke up."

Ron snorted. "You could set your watch by their breakups."

Marcus was torn. He didn't want to chase away the hottest girl who had ever been interested in him. On the flip side, it was hard enough to be the new guy with a tight-knit unit like the Raiders when the team captain's ex *wasn't* hitting on you.

"Hey, stranger!" Alyssa greeted him. "Nice moves out there."

He grimaced. "They still drop my passes unless Coach is on their necks."

She looked him up and down. "I wasn't following the *ball*."

Marcus shuffled uncomfortably. "Listen, maybe we should keep a low profile around practice when—you know—the guys are watching."

She regarded him pityingly. "When you throw off your back foot, you can't get any zip in your passes."

Summer practices ended by noon. That day, driving with one hand and wolfing down his sandwich with the other, Marcus headed straight for Three Alarm Park as his new routine dictated. Whatever Charlie had meant by "the usual," the newest Raider didn't want to be late for the more important half of his football education.

As it happened, "the usual" seemed to mean "whenever I show up—*if* I show up." There were days when Marcus would have to kill three hours before Charlie came jogging down the path. There were days when the man never turned up at all. And there were times when Marcus would kill the motor on his bike to find Charlie already draped over the Paper Airplane, genuinely miffed at being kept waiting. "Where were you?" he'd say. "Having lunch with the president? I've been here forever!"

At first, Marcus had tried to formalize their schedule, but it just didn't seem to work. Charlie would readily agree to meet at twelve thirty, and then the next day, he'd roll in at quarter to four without so much as an excuse. *Plan? What plan?*

It was annoying, but waiting to see if Charlie was going to show up soon became Marcus's personal reality TV show. In an odd way, the introduction of this random factor somehow made his life richer. Charlie wasn't boring, that was for sure.

Of course, now that Marcus trained with Charlie, he had very little enthusiasm for running down his own passes when he was training alone. The solitary workouts got lamer and lamer until they began to resemble vigils for the missing fifty-something man.

He was more than happy to stop what he was doing when a voice from outside the park called, "Hey!"

"Charlie?" This was new. One of the few predictable things about the man was that he usually entered Three Alarm Park from the west path.

"Are you Marcus Jordan?"

Marcus peered through a gap in the greenery. A tall, cadaverous man in dark green coveralls was waving for his attention. *One of Barker's assistants?* he wondered.

Who else knew him in Kennesaw?

"That's me."

In reply, the man simply turned on his heel and marched away, disappearing behind the foliage.

Confused, Marcus ran after him. "Wait—I'm Marcus!"

But by the time he could make it to a park exit, the man was gone. Instead, standing thirty feet in front of him was Charlie.

"Hey, Mac—you going to stand there all day, or are you going to throw me the ball?"

In their evolving parlance, that was actually an invitation to drill it at his face. Marcus cocked back and unloaded with full power. Charlie got his quick hands up and caught it a split second before it would have pushed his nose out the back of his skull.

Charlie could opt for a return missile, but he generally lobbed the ball back high and slow. The old guy had the timing down pat so he could charge Marcus and level him the instant his fingers touched pigskin.

The pain was unbelievable, but there was something about these workouts that Marcus couldn't duplicate anywhere else. No one on the Raiders could hit like Charlie. It wasn't just the brute force he used but the technique. When Charlie made contact, he didn't just knock you down; he sent you in a specific direction, propelling you exactly where he wanted you to land. He used his own body as a piece of equipment, the way a tennis player used a racket. It jarred your teeth, but it also opened your eyes.

Back in Kansas, Marcus had always looked upon the physical contact as a necessary evil—something to be avoided and occasionally endured in the course of the pure passing game. For Charlie, the contact *was* the game. Not only did he love the "pop," he understood it, the way Einstein understood the space-time continuum. It was like the guy was a professor of tackling. And in the same way a good teacher can transmit his love of the topic to his students, Charlie's enthusiasm for smashmouth football was beginning to rub off on Marcus.

A hit used to mean failure and heading back to the drawing board. Now Marcus was starting to anticipate the contact, analyze it, and make split-second adjustments so the collision could be advantageous to him. And once he saw that there could be advantage in it, the fear faded, and he began almost to look forward to it. The pain was still there—doled out by Charlie, there was pain to spare. But it was exhilarating. It made him feel totally in the game and in the moment. It made him feel alive.

Mom had begun asking about the profusion of cuts and bruises. "When you played football in Olathe, you didn't come home all beat up every day."

"That was JV—*junior*." There were many words to describe Charlie, but junior wasn't any of them.

Anyway, Charlie seemed to be as good at administering first aid as he was at creating the need for it. They were constantly leaving the park for ice, bandages, and rubbing alcohol. And Gatorade in large quantities.

In town, everyone they met greeted Charlie by name and seemed genuinely happy to run into him. For his part, Charlie was affable, friendly, even charming. But he never stopped to talk to anybody.

At the pharmacy, Charlie loaded his arms with drinks, PowerBars, and first-aid supplies. Then he breezed blithely out the door, not paying a cent for anything, as usual.

The man at the register just chuckled and made a note on a ring-bound pad. "Have a good one, Charlie!"

Marcus must have looked bewildered, because the cashier explained, "His wife comes by over the weekend and settles up. Don't sweat it. You get used to Charlie."

Okay, Charlie had a wife. Marcus tucked away that piece of information and hoped to be able to add to it.

The end of a workout was just as unpredictable as the beginning. Charlie might suddenly say, "I've got to go," or "See you tomorrow." A couple of afternoons, he headed for the park exit without a single word.

At first, Marcus wondered what triggered the impulse for his training companion to leave. It didn't seem to be the hour. Charlie wore an expensive-looking gold watch, but he never once consulted it. Maybe the guy went by his stomach—when he got hungry, it was time to go home for dinner.

That afternoon, though, it was Marcus who shut

things down. "Listen, I'd better head home. My mom gets nuts if she thinks I'm AWOL."

Charlie nodded sympathetically. "Yeah, mine, too."

Marcus laughed. "Your wife, you mean."

"Right . . . ," Charlie said and walked away.

In the parking lot, Marcus packed up his gear, slung his duffel over his shoulder, and mounted the scooter.

"Marcus Jordan?"

He wheeled to face the same cadaverous man, tall and skinny, with a long pointy nose. K.O. PEST CONTROL was embroidered on the breast pocket of his coveralls. Standing beside him, blocking the Vespa's exit, was a uniformed cop.

"Here," Marcus said.

"I told you it's him!" the man in coveralls exclaimed. "He's the one who vandalized my car!"

Marcus was aghast. "It was an accident! I left a note!"

"He admits it!" crowed the exterminator. He reached into one of his many pockets and drew out a folded piece of paper. He opened it to reveal the letter Marcus had left on the dashboard of the Toyota.

Sorry for the damage. Will pay to fix.
Marcus Jordan 555-7385

"Very funny, kid," the needle-nosed man growled. "You know how many times I called that number? The teachers at the preschool were ready to kill me!"

"I'm sorry!" Marcus was chagrined. "I messed up my number. We just moved here."

"That's convenient."

"It's the truth!"

The officer sighed. "All right, Marcus. Looks like you're coming with me."

Barbara Jordan rushed into the police station and joined her son at the officer's desk.

"This is all a misunderstanding," she tried to explain. "Marcus has never been in any trouble."

"He still hasn't," the officer assured her. "I think we've got it sorted out. Broken car window, wrong number on the note. It also clears up a crank call complaint from Growing Minds Preschool. The gals over there don't have much of a sense of humor when the phone rings during naptime."

"It was an honest mistake," Marcus pleaded.

"Sounds like it," the cop agreed. "Just pay Mr. Oliver to fix his window and we'll forget the whole thing."

"I'll take care of it," promised Mrs. Jordan. "We just moved here. We really don't want to get off on the wrong foot."

"Smart." The officer swiveled in his chair to face Marcus's mother. "Guess I'm not much of a welcome wagon. Mike Deluca." He held out his hand.

She shook it. "Barbara Jordan. I work at the *Advocate*.

And Marcus just made the Raiders. He plays quarterback."

The officer smiled. "We've been looking for someone to back Troy up. Just keep those passes on target. Lot of car windows around town."

Outside the station house, Mrs. Jordan let out a long breath. "That could have been a lot worse."

Marcus flushed. "I feel bad about the wrong number, but that guy Oliver's a jerk. He wanted to press charges! Thank God that cop was cool about it."

"He's nice," his mother agreed. "The last thing you need is a bad reputation in a new town. I hope you're watching your speed on that rocket sled Dad bought you."

"I keep a line of grannies riding up my tail," Marcus promised.

"How did you break this man's window, anyway?"

Marcus shrugged uncomfortably. "Playing football in the park."

"Why would you throw a football at a parked car?"

"Another guy threw it," Marcus admitted. "It went through my hands."

"Another guy?" she repeated. "You're moaning and groaning about how the team hates you, and all this time you've been meeting a friend to play football?"

"He's not a friend," Marcus said quickly. "He's just some guy I ran into in the park. I really don't know much about him."

She digested this. "Well, if he threw the pass, shouldn't *his* mother be writing the check?"

A mirthless smile twitched Marcus's lips at the thought of Charlie's mother, undoubtedly a little old lady in her seventies or eighties, paying for her son's share of the damage.

"We'll split it," he decided. "Fair enough?"

She put an arm around his shoulder. "Fair enough. Do you want me to call over to his house, or can you handle it?"

"I'll handle it."

But could he? Never once had he seen Charlie handing over money—not even for a lousy bag of ice or a bottle of Gatorade. Could Marcus get him to pay for half a car window that had been broken more than a week ago?

And more important, if Charlie stonewalled him, what did that mean for the workouts in Three Alarm Park?

The blond cocker spaniel jumped off the porch and bounded over to greet Charlie, tail wagging.

He reached down to pet the animal. "How're you doing, Boomer? Good boy." He followed the dog to the screen door.

A teenage girl was there to let them in. "Hi, Daddy," she said, kissing Charlie on the cheek. "What did you do today?"

"Threw a ball around," her father replied.

"With who?"

Charlie shrugged. "The cops came and arrested him." He headed into the kitchen.

Fifteen-year-old Chelsea turned to her brother. "Troy, did you hear that?"

Troy looked away from the Aldrich Raiders playbook. "I try not to listen to Dad anymore."

She looked worried. "Do you think it's getting worse?"

Troy's All-American features tightened. "Worse than going crazy?"

"He's *not* crazy. You understand exactly what's happening to him. It's not his fault."

Troy turned back to his playbook. "Like that makes any difference."

Chelsea sighed. "Yeah, I know what you mean." She filled a bowl with dry dog food and whistled for the spaniel. "Come on, Silky. Here's your dinner, girl."

CHAPTER FIVE

The classroom numbers at David Nathan Aldrich High School defied the laws of science.

Marcus followed the progression: 238 . . . 239 . . . 240 . . . B-611? Confused, he stared from the schedule in his hand to the number over the door and back to the schedule again. History was supposed to be meeting in room 241. Where was that? Up on the roof?

"Very hot—kind of Lost Puppy meets Dumb Jock."

Alyssa appeared at his elbow, all sympathy.

Her presence brought out a definite nervousness in Marcus. What could you make of a girl who could flirt with you one minute and criticize the cadence of your snap count the next? He could still feel her arms around his midsection from their Vespa ride—or was that just wishful thinking?

"I'm having a little trouble with the layout of the building," he admitted.

She nodded in understanding. "All the new kids stall out at B-611. I figured I'd find you here sooner or later."

"Are you going to tell me where to go or what?"

She laughed. "I'll leave that to Troy. He's dying for the chance to tell you where to go."

"Yeah, thanks for that," Marcus muttered.

Alyssa shook her head. "Don't blame me. Football's a zero-sum game. More wannabes than positions. Your success always costs some other guy his job."

"Yeah, well, Troy is job security personified," Marcus complained. "The players take their orders from Troy, not from the coach. And even *he* wishes I'd play JV and make everybody's life easier."

"You don't know what it was like last season."

He was disgusted. "Sacrilegious as it may seem, the Raiders aren't the only high school squad that ever won a championship."

She was patient. "When you love a team—I mean *really* love it—your whole life is about two words: *if only*. If only Kevin could get bigger; if only Luke could get faster; if only Ron could stop fumbling. Some of it's coaching, but mostly it's an act of God. Last year, the Raiders hit the *if only* jackpot. All our potential cashed in at the same time—especially Troy. He rewrote the record book. Even better, most of our *if only*s were juniors, so ninety percent of them are back. Now enter this kid on a goofy scooter, saying he's better than the team that went eleven and oh—"

"I never said that!" Marcus interrupted hotly.

"In their minds you did. These guys have put so much pressure on themselves that *everything* is about them and their season."

Marcus was already sick of hearing about the Raiders' chance at history. Wasting precious Alyssa time on the subject was a crime against humanity. "So where *is* Troy? You're with me, so I assume he's watching from a distance. Or is it enough if he hears about it from a third party?"

She bristled. "Is that what you think this is?" She pulled him into room B-611, stood up on her toes, and kissed him.

"There," she breathed. "No P.R. value at all."

The lights came on suddenly, and someone entered the room, catching them with their arms wrapped around each other.

The girl glared at them in disapproval. "You have got to be kidding me!"

"This is none of your business, Chelsea," Alyssa said defensively. "You know Troy and I broke up."

"For which minute?" Chelsea sneered. "Oh, sorry— it only takes you that long to find somebody new." She looked scornfully at Marcus. "Do you know who you're dealing with? Or can't you get past the pom-poms and the short skirt?"

"*You're* someone to lecture *me* on the rules of dating," Alyssa accused, "considering you've never gone out with anybody in your life."

"Yeah, and if being like you and Troy is what I have to look forward to," Chelsea shot back, "then I never want to." She wished Marcus a sarcastic "Good luck—you'll need it!" and stormed out.

"Who's that?" he asked.

"Chelsea Popovich."

"Troy's sister?"

She nodded grimly. "Not one of my fans."

Chelsea was obviously just showing loyalty to her jilted brother. Marcus thought back to what Ron had said that day at practice: *You could set your watch by their breakups.*

"Are you and Troy really broken up, or is this—you know—part of the dance?"

She reddened. "It did happen that way a couple of times. But a few months ago, Troy *changed*. It wasn't only with me. He got just as weird with his friends. Troy's house used to be the hangout spot. Now he's always on his own. Maybe it's the stress of trying to repeat this season. . . ." She made a face. "You know, Marcus, you're a dope. Do you really think talking about this is going to get you any action?"

The second bell rang. They were both officially late.

He had to ask. "Action . . . ?"

She pointed out the door. "Room 241—three doors down, after the custodian's closet."

K.O. Pest Control was a storefront operation on Poplar Street, which bordered the east side of Three Alarm Park.

Marcus propped his bike on its kickstand and approached the entrance gingerly. The giant metal cockroach that hung over the front door wasn't exactly welcoming. But the needle-nosed face that appeared was even less so.

"You! What do you want?"

Marcus held out a white envelope containing his mother's check for $310 in payment for the broken window. "I brought your money, Mr. Oliver. Like I said before, sorry about what happened."

The exterminator tore open the seal and examined the contents carefully. "I hope this is better than the telephone number you gave me."

Marcus swallowed an angry retort. *This guy may be an idiot, but he didn't ask to have his window broken.*

"Anyway, I'm glad there are no hard feelings."

"You kids kill me," Oliver snarled. "It's no big deal to bust things up, but when it's time to pay for what you've done, you run straight to Mommy."

Marcus took a deep breath. "Well, I don't have that kind of money, so if you want to get paid, you'd better take it from my mom."

"Are you trying to be smart with me?" Oliver demanded.

"I can't believe you!" Marcus finally exploded. "I could have run away after I broke your window! But I did the right thing—and now you're *insulting* me for it?"

"You punk!" the exterminator roared. "Get away from my place of business. Who do you think you are? I never want to see you—"

From out of nowhere, a clod of earth sailed through the air and made violent contact with the giant metal cockroach over the door. It exploded into a million pieces, raining dirt and bits of grass down on Kenneth Oliver. He glared at Marcus in outrage.

"You can't blame that on me," Marcus defended himself. "I'm standing right here in front of you."

"You think I'm stupid?" the exterminator sputtered. "You lousy kids run in packs! For all I know, every tree on this block has one of your delinquent friends crouched behind it!"

"What friends?" Marcus demanded. "Everyone in town is about as welcoming as *you*!" And he stormed away, boiling with fury. If he stuck around, he'd only end up with Officer Deluca again. Sixteen years in Olathe had produced fewer ugly confrontations than Marcus had experienced during less than a month in photogenic Kennesaw.

Troy and his minions were bad enough, but this guy Oliver was a new low. How paranoid did you have to be to believe that Marcus had packed the street with hidden accomplices preparing to unleash an artillery barrage of dirt bombs?

"Mac—over here."

"Huh?" Marcus looked around. There, concealed in the brush at the edge of Three Alarm Park, was Charlie.

Instantly, he knew whose unerring arm had thrown the missile.

"What were you doing over there with Old Man Dingley?" Charlie whispered loudly.

"Paying for the window *you* broke," Marcus shot back. "And who's Dingley? The guy's name is Kenneth Oliver. Your half comes to a hundred and fifty-five bucks, by the way."

"No problem," Charlie said airily.

"Yes problem. My mom laid out that cash, and she has to get paid back. It doesn't have to be this minute, but it has to be."

"Done," Charlie murmured absently, but his eyes never left Kenneth Oliver's storefront across the street. "That guy needs to be taught a lesson."

"I got hauled in by the cops because of him. Do me a favor—no more bombing his pest-control shop."

"Pest control," Charlie mused. "That makes it easy. We'll sugar him."

Marcus was dubious. "Sugar him?"

Charlie nodded. "He's a bug killer. Let's give him some bugs to kill."

■ ■ ■

The next thing he knew, Marcus was following Charlie down the condiment aisle of the supermarket, his arms laden. "Okay, we've got honey, molasses, and chocolate syrup. What's next?"

"Sugar," Charlie replied, hefting a large bag. "Ten pounds ought to do it."

"Ten pounds!" Marcus echoed. "We'll attract every insect in the state!"

The older man shrugged. "I'm sure there are a couple of stink bugs in Syracuse who won't bother making the trip."

Marcus started for the checkout counter, but he already knew no money would be changing hands. The cashier made a few notes and waved him along after Charlie, who was already striding through the automatic door.

Bearing their purchases, they retreated to the park to wait for Kenneth Oliver to close up shop for the day. They had no football with them, so the workout consisted purely of hitting. It was brutal, and yet there was a beautiful simplicity to it—the jarring collision of muscle on muscle, bone on bone. Marcus was never wide-awake like he was when he felt that full-speed contact. Not even when throwing a touchdown pass.

It was only during their brief breaks that Marcus allowed his gaze—and his doubts—to settle on the supermarket bags leaning against the *Remembrance* sculpture. Why would a grown man get involved in somebody else's payback prank? Involved, hell—this whole thing was Charlie's idea! What was in it for him?

At the same time, he felt strangely honored that his companion was so dead set on revenge on his behalf. Did the guy consider the two of them such good friends that any insult to Marcus was an insult to Charlie, too? There was nothing halfway about the way they played football together. But beyond that, they were strangers separated by four decades.

Marcus couldn't shake the feeling that this was probably a *very* bad idea. He ought to back away. Yet, at the close of the afternoon, he found himself crouched in the bushes beside Charlie, watching as the exterminator locked the front door of the shop, got into his Toyota, and drove off.

"All right," Marcus announced. "You're the big expert on sugaring. How do we do this?"

Charlie had the whole thing planned out in the time it took them to cross the street from Three Alarm Park. First he removed the weather stripping that sealed the bottom of the door. Then he squeezed a long line of honey across the crack.

Marcus watched, fascinated. The man worked with the delicate touch of a surgeon, but there was something more—an athlete's ability to focus with unwavering concentration. Charlie sugared a store with the same tunnel vision he brought to his beloved "pops." His lively blue eyes gleamed with purpose.

Next, he painted the bottom of the door with molasses, all the way to the mail slot, which he propped open with a Popsicle stick.

In spite of everything, Marcus had to smile. "Pretty slick."

"Are you kidding?" Charlie chortled. "We haven't even got to the chocolate sauce yet."

That was next, fanning out from the door in long trails. One curled around the side of the building into the weedy lot behind. Another went across the street, where it broke into tributaries leading into Three Alarm Park. A third led straight down the sewer in the middle of the road.

"What if somebody sees us?" Marcus asked nervously. There were a few people around, but no one was close enough to get much of a look at what they were doing.

Charlie was unperturbed as he worked the squeeze bottle. "Let them."

Marcus could only marvel at his unflappability. This wasn't the kind of tab his wife could stop by and settle up. Sure, it wasn't international terrorism, but Marcus knew one exterminator who was going to be seriously bent out of shape over this.

As they retraced the lines back to the front door, Marcus sprinkled sugar over the chocolate stripes.

"Not too much," Charlie advised. "We don't want it to be too delicious out here. We want to lead them inside for the main banquet." He took the sugar bag from Marcus, inserted the pouring spout into the mail slot, and dumped the remainder of the ten pounds inside the store.

Marcus reached in with a long twig and swept the sugar around, spreading the pile all about the floor.

Charlie rubbed his hands together in anticipation. "Look—ants are already investigating the chocolate syrup. By morning, this place is going to be a bug sanctuary!"

Marcus took note of the store hours posted on the door. "He opens at nine. We should he here by eight thirty."

Charlie nodded. "That guy's going to rue the day he ever messed with us!"

Marcus couldn't escape the suspicion that this episode would provide plenty of ruing to go around.

CHAPTER SIX

When Marcus awoke the next morning, he knew about eight seconds of tranquility before it all came flooding back.

Oh, God.

What a stupid thing to do. What a waste of time and energy, not to mention sugar, syrup, chocolate sauce, and whatever else they'd spread around K.O. Pest Control. He didn't even have the consolation of having been just a spectator. He'd had a million chances to walk away, and yet something had kept him there. There had been no stopping Charlie, but Marcus supposedly had full use of his own free will! And if this prank turned out to be half as awful as he was pretty sure it was going to be . . .

He checked the clock on the nightstand. Six fifty-seven. Getting back to sleep was utterly impossible. He was too stressed. Sixteen years old and playing with bugs. How pathetic was that?

And yet he had to know. Had Charlie's concoction of sugar and spice and all things nice attracted enough insects to freak out an exterminator? The answer was a short ride away.

Downstairs, his mother was loading the pickup truck with tripods and equipment.

She looked at him as he appeared in the front hall. "You're up? You? Rip Van Marcus? What's the occasion?"

"You were up earlier," he pointed out.

"My shift doesn't start till noon, so I thought I'd try to catch the morning light on the Gunks."

That was the mountain range Mom was so hot and bothered about for her book—the Shawangunks, or Gunks for short. It sounded more like what was probably going on inside Kenneth Oliver's mail slot. Marcus flooded a bowl of raisin bran with milk and began to eat, still standing.

"Did you call your father last night?" she asked.

"What should I call him?" he mumbled, mouth full.

She looked at him reproachfully. "He phoned you."

"Must have been a slow day at the Kremlin."

She grew tight-lipped. "If you don't return the

call, sooner or later I'll get a lawyer's letter accusing me of alienating him from his child. He, who invented alienation."

"I'll e-mail," Marcus offered. "I've got a busy day."

"It's Saturday. What are you so busy about?"

I'm meeting my middle-aged friend down at the bug infestation. Aloud, he murmured something about homework and football and Three Alarm Park.

She shouldered her camera bag. "Make the call," she said. "And not because I don't want to get served. You only get one father."

He watched her climb into the truck and drive away. She had guts, his mother, and not just for betting her professional future on a mountain range with a dumb name. He was almost in awe of her determination to succeed—Marcus didn't care that much about anything, except maybe football. Guts *and* character. She had more reason to hate Comrade Stalin than anybody. She knew that the phone conversation would be chock-full of glitzy, expensive inducements for Marcus to abandon her and move back to Kansas. Surely it had crossed her mind that one day her ex might dream up a carrot to dangle that Marcus couldn't resist. Yet she never let her son write the guy off.

Still, Marcus wasn't planning to call. Not on Bug Day. He wolfed down the rest of the cereal, scrambled into some clothes, and jumped on the Vespa, heading downtown.

He parked on the next block over and had to keep

himself from sprinting all the way to K.O. Pest Control. Stupid, maybe, but now that it was a done deal, the suspense was killing him. He approached the store gingerly, trying not to step on the many ants swarming around the chocolate trails. Sure, there were a lot of bugs outside. The question was, had they gone in?

The early-morning sun streaming through the small window in the door provided the answer. The inside of the shop was alive. He couldn't see the floor for the black seething mass that covered it. And not just ants, either. There were June bugs, beetles, earwigs, ladybugs, caterpillars, grasshoppers, crickets, cockroaches, fleas, and spiders of all varieties. Flies, moths, and mosquitoes swooped and hovered. The walls crawled.

Marcus remembered from a science class in middle school that there were more than 800,000 species of insects. He was pretty sure that most of them were represented inside K.O. Pest Control that morning. If Kenneth Oliver enjoyed his work, he was in for a treat.

So was Charlie.

It probably wasn't a good idea to be seen hanging around the store on a day when neighbors and passersby might be asked if they'd seen anything suspicious. So he retreated to Three Alarm Park to await the arrival of his partner in crime.

It was just after eight—plenty of time to kill. He tried to catnap on a bench, without success. A few laps of the park were a good warm-up, but for what? He couldn't exactly tackle himself. He even tried to climb the flukes of the Paper Airplane and was gratified to note that the smooth granite didn't defeat him quite so easily anymore. It was a fringe benefit of his physical combat with Charlie. He was developing a lower center of gravity, which enhanced his sense of balance. He was going to be tough to bring down this season—if Coach Barker ever let him touch the ball.

He looked at his watch again. Eight thirty-five. Where was Charlie? Surely he wouldn't plan such an elaborate prank and then not show up for the payoff. The guy was inconsistent in his arrival time for training, but this was different, wasn't it?

He left the park and began to pace along Poplar Street. A few of the stores had opened, but there was still no sign of Kenneth Oliver.

And still no Charlie.

"There's a good spot, Daddy."

Following his daughter's direction, Charlie pulled his car up to the curb in front of the cell phone store.

"Thanks." Chelsea got out. "I just have to pick up my phone. It should only take a couple of minutes. Don't get out of the car, okay? Here—listen to some music." She reached in through the open passenger window and switched on the radio.

Charlie regarded her peevishly. "I'm not an idiot. You don't have to tell me every little thing."

"I know. I'm sorry."

She entered the store and approached the repair desk, keeping one eye on the display window and Charlie in the parked car outside. She felt odd treating her father like an eight-year-old, but the alternative wasn't fun to contemplate.

Anyway, she reflected with a little embarrassment, her father wasn't the one who'd thrown jeans in the wash without taking the cell phone out of the pocket.

"Good news—we just had to change the battery," the man told her. "No permanent damage."

"Thanks." She handed over some bills and accepted the protective pouch containing her phone.

"Say hi to your dad for me," he called after her.

Always to Dad. Oh, they knew Mom existed, but she wasn't the one who mattered.

She exited the store and froze. The car was still parked out front. The driver's-side door was wide open, blocking half the lane.

Her father was gone.

Marcus watched the exterminator's Camry turn onto Poplar and ease into a parking space near K.O. Pest Control.

He couldn't believe it. Charlie wasn't going to show up for his own prank.

And suddenly, there he was, ambling aimlessly like this wasn't three seconds to Zero Hour.

Marcus raced down the street, grabbed his partner

in crime by the arm, and began hauling him along the sidewalk.

Charlie shoved him away with such force that Marcus very nearly tumbled to the pavement.

"He's parking his car!" Marcus urged. "We're going to miss it!"

This galvanized Charlie's attention. "Lead the way!" He matched the teenager stride for stride, following him to a good vantage point behind a parked truck.

Oliver was out of his Camry, heading for the front door. His key reached for the lock.

"Daddy?" Chelsea ran up, the cell phone pouch still in her hand. She gawked at Marcus like he was an extinct reptile reborn and wreaking havoc on the streets of Kennesaw. "You!"

The exterminator opened the door and took a step inside his shop. Even from behind the truck, they could hear the sickening crunch of his shoe on the floor.

His howl of revulsion and shock cut through the morning like an air-raid siren. He backed out of the store on high-stepping feet, his head obscured by a cloud of flies and moths.

Charlie let out a whoop of merriment. "Sugared!"

A bubble of laughter burst from Marcus. "Big-time."

Chelsea's eyes widened in outrage. "You've got no business involving my father—"

"Involving?" Marcus cut her off. "The whole thing was his idea! He's the one involving me!"

She took Charlie's arm and pulled him onto the sidewalk. "Stay away from him!" she rasped to Marcus. "You have no clue who you're dealing with! This is our family's private business!" To her father she said, "Come on, Daddy, let's go."

Marcus waited for Charlie to put his big-mouth daughter in her place. Where did she get off telling this force of nature, who delivered hits like a rhino and scampered up fences and statues like it was nothing, what to do and who to associate with?

Charlie never said a word. To be fair, he was distracted by the spectacle of Kenneth Oliver trying to slap-dance the insects off his shoes and clothing. But he followed Chelsea almost meekly.

Marcus retreated to the cover of the park, the shine gone from his revenge. Chelsea's scorn ate at him. Like he was running around recruiting people's fathers to hang out with. Like he'd even heard of "sugaring" before Charlie. Charlie *Popovich*.

Well, that was his name, right? Chelsea was Troy's sister. And that meant Charlie was Troy's dad.

Didn't it figure? A jerk like Troy got the world's greatest natural athlete for a father. Comrade Stalin's sport of choice was barking orders at people, aided by a bullhorn voice and the unshakable belief that he was right about every subject, one hundred percent of the time.

Come to think of it, Stalin could probably take a few lessons from Chelsea. She wasn't exactly a charm school graduate, and she was pushy enough to make her father late for his own prank. Troy was obviously a major idiot, so if Mrs. Popovich was anything like her kids, no wonder Charlie was a little unfocused.

Marcus's brow clouded. That still didn't explain the shove. Sure, Charlie was a physical guy, but that was no friendly straight-arm. That was a genuine *get-out-of-my-face*. A few seconds later he was the same old Charlie, but at that moment he'd been a stranger—and not a very pleasant one at that.

Charlie Popovich—why did that name sound familiar? *Football* familiar . . .

Chelsea's words came back to him: *You have no clue who you're dealing with.*

Maybe it was time to get a clue.

CHAPTER SEVEN

$\mathbb{G}$oogle churned up more than 46,000 hits on the keywords *Charlie Popovich*.

Marcus sat forward in his desk chair. After the hours he'd spent wondering about the mysterious Charlie, he'd never expected the guy's life story to be so easy to find. Eagerly, he clicked on the top link.

It was an article from the sports section of the *Cincinnati Inquirer* of February 18, 1991:

BENGALS' "KING OF POP" HANGS UP CLEATS

Charlie Popovich has informed the Cincinnati Bengals organization of his retirement at age 36 after fourteen seasons, seven of those with the Bengals. The six-foot-three, 235-pound linebacker was credited with 1,097 career tackles, including 754 solo stops, 22.5 sacks, and seven interceptions.

Originally selected by the San Diego Chargers in the 1977 NFL draft, the King of Pop soon became known throughout the league as a tenacious defender with a relish for intense physical contact. At the same time, Popovich developed a reputation both in San Diego and Cincinnati as a locker-room prankster, making him beloved and often feared by teammates and coaches alike. . . .

Marcus exhaled sharply and realized he'd been holding his breath. Unbelievable. For the past three weeks, he'd been bashing heads with a former NFL linebacker! The King of Pop! Not a superstar, exactly, but a solid player with a fourteen-year career.

I should have known, Marcus thought. No wonder Charlie was still such an athletic force. No wonder he could dish out hits like cluster bombs, even at his age. Marcus did the math. The veteran was in his mid-fifties by now. This also explained why Charlie had so much free time in the middle of the day. He wasn't unemployed; he was *retired.* And probably pretty flush, too. The money in pro sports wasn't as huge as it was today, but even in the seventies and eighties, NFL players were pretty well paid.

Enough to splurge for half a car window, that's for sure.

Marcus browsed through the other links. Most were just game coverage, with the occasional mention of a play Charlie had been involved in. There were a few articles about charity work he'd done in San Diego and Cincinnati, as well as a *Sports Illustrated* piece: "Rookies to Watch in 1977." Marcus drank it all in, mesmerized. Charlie had never made a Pro Bowl, but he had started for most of his fourteen seasons and had always found a way to be an impact player.

There was a picture of him in action, circa 1983. He was in full flight, his body parallel to the turf, tackling Joe Theismann of the Washington Redskins. The impact of the collision had knocked Charlie's helmet clean off. The photograph captured it in midair two feet behind him, revealing a face Marcus would have recognized anywhere. Charlie was younger, the tousled hair black instead of salt and pepper, but the sharp eyes and laser-focus concentration were unmistakable. The guy might have aged a quarter century, but his love of competition hadn't faded one bit.

Sometimes you actually hear it go pop! There was little question that the tackle in the photograph had been one of those times. Marcus heard it, too, and felt the devastating collision he'd experienced so many times in his encounters with Charlie.

He closed the computer's browser and leaned back in

his chair. All this time he'd been training one-on-one with a real NFL veteran, and he'd been too clueless to know it. He couldn't wait to get back to Three Alarm Park—to get hit again like Joe Theismann and countless other players from the seventies and eighties.

He couldn't wait for his next pop.

"This is your huddle, Jordan!" the coach bellowed from the sidelines. "You've got to take charge!"

Barker was always raving about the role of quarterback as field general, but Marcus knew better. As Ron had put it, "To these guys, you're never going to be any more than a buck private on recruiting day."

Of course, Ron himself was part of that elite group, but at least the halfback was pretty cool about it—which was more than you could say for most of the Raiders, and a hell of a lot more than you could say for Troy.

The snap was lame and mistimed, but Marcus had gotten good at controlling it. *One benefit of being toe jam,* thought Marcus, *is that you learn to handle adversity.*

The offensive line evaporated in a heartbeat, and pass rushers were after him. His teammates never offered him any protection, but when it came to tackling him, their enthusiasm knew no bounds.

"You're dropping back too far, Jordan!" brayed the coach.

No, I'm fleeing for my life! he thought, scrambling madly. But Barker was right. He was going to take a shot anyway. The only question was, could he do his job before he got slammed?

Caught in the crosshairs of the charging linebacker, he squared up and threw. The defender struck just at the moment of release, with Marcus's arm extended, his body exposed and vulnerable. The collision drove him backward, sprawling.

As he hit the turf, it came to him: This was *nothing*! If that had been Charlie, he'd be five yards away, still vibrating, waiting for the fireworks display in his brain to come into focus. He scrambled up to see Luke, the intended receiver, running downfield with the ball.

Barker blew the whistle, and the play broke up amid a smattering of applause from the handful of students in the bleachers.

"Next time, try not to run like a scared rabbit first," he grunted.

"Got it. Thanks, Coach." There was a compliment hidden in there somewhere, even if it was unspoken.

Marcus felt a slap on his shoulder pads and turned to peer into the faceguard of the linebacker who had decked him.

"I should have pulled up," the kid said apologetically. "My bad."

"Don't worry about it," Marcus told him. "Nice tackle."

At the Gatorade bucket, he found himself next to Troy. He had little contact with Number Seven during practice, and it wasn't because the two of them couldn't stand each other. Generally, Troy trained with the offensive starters, while Marcus took most of his snaps with his fellow backups. Marcus also worked out with the defensive backs. Troy had no official second job, although Ron said the coach used him on special teams here and there.

"Guess I was the only person in town who didn't know who your dad is," Marcus offered.

Troy cast him a look of distaste. "Yeah, I heard you two are playmates."

Marcus bristled. "I'm just trying to tell you what a great guy he is. The stuff he's taught me about football is pure gold."

"He's not your coach," Troy told him. "He's not your friend. Stay away from him."

"Shouldn't that be Charlie's call?" Marcus demanded.

"Charlie's call." Troy laughed bitterly. "You don't even know what that means."

"You talk like I'm a stalker! It's totally random that I met your old man. But you know what? I'm glad it happened, because just about everybody else in this town treats me like crap—especially you! God knows how someone as cool as Charlie wound up with two kids like you and Miss Congeniality!" And he stormed off, fuming.

After practice, Marcus was certain he was about to be fed to the locker-room toilet. But Troy kept his anger to himself. A few of the players even complimented Marcus on a good workout. Maybe freedom of speech wasn't dead on this team after all.

He was toweling his hair dry after the shower when he heard the rustling of pom-poms outside the locker hut. He hoisted himself up to the transom window and peered down.

Alyssa. Every time he found himself lamenting the move from Kansas, she was his go-to thought. There was nobody like Alyssa at his old school, nobody even close. Stalin there, Alyssa here—it was all the marketing campaign the Kennesaw Chamber of Commerce could've asked for.

He was about to call down to her when a figure approached. Troy.

"You're here late."

"You looked good today," Alyssa praised him. "Nice mobility in the pocket."

Marcus felt an odd twinge of jealousy. He'd thought he was the sole recipient of her scouting reports.

"Do you ever turn it off?" Troy asked in annoyance.

"What, in football season?"

He sighed. "Come on, I'll give you a ride home."

"That's okay. I'll hang out."

The great Troy Popovich wasn't used to being told no, even by his ex.

"You're waiting for *him*, aren't you?"

"Who?" she asked innocently.

"I'm not a moron, Lyss! He's the only guy left in the locker room!"

She bristled. "He has a name, Troy. So what if I'm going with Marcus?"

"Is this supposed to be revenge or something?" he demanded.

"No. I like the guy. The fact that it bugs you is really just a bonus." She shrugged. "I'm a sucker for an arm. Worked for you, remember?"

"He's nothing," Troy scoffed.

"Watch him sometime," Alyssa urged. "You were raw at the beginning of last year, too. Marcus is the real deal."

Apparently, Troy wasn't in the mood for a quarterback comparison. He was gone by the time Marcus dressed and dashed outside.

Alyssa wrapped Marcus's arm around her waist and started in the direction of the school. "You're driving me home on your mean set of wheels."

"Where do you live?"

"Why do guys have to be so practical? It's not the destination, it's the *journey*. Although," she added skeptically, "the Barney-Davidson doesn't give us much room to work with."

They walked in lockstep for a while, like a slow-motion three-legged race. Then Marcus asked, "Why is Troy so weird about Charlie?"

She rolled her eyes. "You're obviously a newbie at this

boyfriend-girlfriend thing. Basically, you're supposed to be getting me all hot and bothered. So why don't you try a new topic?"

But Marcus was determined to learn the truth. "It can't just be that Troy hates me, because Chelsea's the same way. What's up with that family?"

Alyssa was impatient. "I can't think of anybody who doesn't have issues with their parents. Don't you?"

"Sure. Half the reason I'm here is to get away from my dad. But this is different. Charlie's not just an NFL vet, he's awesome. If he was my father, I'd want the whole world to know. But with those two, it's almost like he's a deep, dark secret."

"You've got it wrong," she told him. "Troy worships his dad."

"At tryouts, he nearly bit Kevin's head off for even mentioning the guy."

"It wasn't always that way," she explained. "Troy and Charlie used to be closer than close—watching football, talking football, playing football. I don't know what changed. Maybe this perfect-season stuff has something to do with it. It's a lot of anxiety for the team—especially Troy."

"Right," Marcus said sarcastically. "What's a fourteen-year NFL career compared with setting a record in high school?"

She laughed. "He's not your favorite person. I get that. But he isn't Darth Vader either. Show a little gratitude. If

Troy didn't go all hermit, you wouldn't be here with *moi*."
She tightened her hold on his midsection.

They rounded the corner of the building, and the parking lot came into view. Marcus's anticipation of the next hour popped like a soap bubble. Perched on the Vespa's seat was Officer Deluca.

He said, "The Sugar Plum Fairy, I presume."

As it turned out, Marcus was still able to give Alyssa a lift home that day—in the back of the squad car that was taking him in.

CHAPTER EIGHT

Barbara Jordan arrived at the police station to be greeted by a familiar sight—her son being interrogated by Officer Deluca.

"Sorry to drag you down here," the cop apologized. "I loved your shots of the firehouse fundraiser. The *Advocate* used to print pictures of fingers and thumbs. Nice to know the town paper is stepping up."

"Thank you." She smiled politely, then wheeled toward her son. "Marcus, what's this all about?"

Marcus remained silent, so Deluca filled Mrs. Jordan in on the details of the sugaring of K.O. Pest Control, including some colorful descriptions of "a writhing mountain of insects a foot deep," and "a creeping, buzzing, chirping sound you hear in your innards."

Marcus spoke up at last. "It wasn't all me, Mom. I was just helping the main guy who did it."

The officer nodded understandingly. "See, I believe that. But you've got to give me a name. Unless I know the identity of this 'main guy,' you're him."

"I can't tell you."

"Was it the girl?" Deluca probed. "She's a cute one—is that who you're covering for?"

"No—definitely not Alyssa."

Mrs. Jordan regarded her son sternly. "Marcus, you're protecting someone who's letting you take the blame. And I'm assuming it's the same boy who stuck us with the entire cost of that window."

Marcus set his jaw and said nothing. Who would believe the truth—that the "boy" in question was actually the town celebrity, a middle-aged man with two kids in high school? Not to mention that if he ratted Charlie out, the training sessions in the park, which had done so much to elevate Marcus's play, would be ancient history. No, better to keep quiet.

"Don't be stupid," Deluca argued. "If I don't have another name, I've got no choice in the matter. You'll have to take the whole rap."

"What exactly is this rap you're talking about?" Mrs. Jordan asked.

He sighed heavily. "In this case, probably nothing.

But only because Mr. Oliver is an exterminator. The last thing he wants is to show the whole town that he can't handle a few bugs—or a few million. You can see his problem. Now, here's *your* problem, Marcus. You've paid for the window, and you seem to have lucked out on this one. I know you're new in town, but that's all the free ride you get in Kennesaw. Anything else happens—if Mr. Oliver so much as stubs his toe and you're responsible— you're looking at arrest, prosecution, the whole nine yards. Don't think that just because this guy is a square peg, he doesn't get the full protection of the law. Stay away from him."

"He will. That's something I personally guarantee," Marcus's mother said, narrowing her eyes at her son. "Even if I have to nail him to his bed."

"Good to see you again, Mrs. Jordan." Deluca turned to Marcus. "And *you* I never want to see again."

"You won't have any more problems with me," Marcus promised.

For the second time, Mrs. Jordan drove her son from the police station to his Vespa so he could follow her home.

When they arrived at the parking lot, he reached for the handle, but she hit the lock button and regarded him seriously. "All right, I want the truth. Is it this girl? Is that why you won't tell me what's going on—you don't want me to know you've got a girlfriend?"

"I don't have a girlfriend," Marcus assured her. "At

least not yet. You're way off base. Alyssa has nothing to do with all this."

"Then who does?" she persisted.

"I have to protect this guy's privacy. Don't worry— he's not a gang member or a drug dealer or anything like that. To be honest, I don't know too much about him."

Just that he's an NFL veteran whose teenage children treat him like a child. True, Charlie wasn't the most mature fifty-four-year-old. But that didn't explain everything.

Not by a long shot.

CHAPTER NINE

Left cornerback.

Coach Barker gave him the news just a few minutes before kickoff. "I told you we're deep. We need help in the backfield, and that's where I'm putting you."

Marcus nodded. "That's great, Coach." It wasn't, but beggars couldn't be choosers. He'd been urged to take a starring role on the JV, and this was what he'd opted for.

The home crowd, packed into the bleachers in blatant defiance of the fire marshal's regulations, was raucously appreciative of their defending champs. No wonder Troy thought he was God's gift. Every Saturday afternoon, the whole town turned out to scream it at him.

As the opening ovation began to die down, a familiar foghorn voice swelled above all the others. Marcus turned sharply in its direction. Charlie. Of course Troy's father would be there to cheer his son on. Beside him stood a slim, attractive blond woman—Mrs. Popovich? So that was who flitted around town, paying off Charlie's bills for Gatorade, bandages, and sugar products. She was probably the person to talk to about $155 for half a car window.

His mind traveled back to Three Alarm Park the other day—his first meeting with Charlie after learning his practice partner's NFL credentials. The man had seemed so flustered at being identified as the King of Pop that Marcus had honestly wondered if he had the wrong person.

"That's you, right? Charlie Popovich of the Chargers and the Bengals?"

"Yeah, sure," he'd replied vaguely, and retreated up the Paper Airplane.

Marcus hadn't broached the subject since. Obviously, Charlie didn't like to discuss his playing days. Maybe there had been an overenthusiastic fan—perhaps more than one. That might explain why Troy and Chelsea were so protective of their dad, and so angry at anyone who approached him.

Playing cornerback was a thankless job. If you made a play, that was just the defense working as it was designed to. If you missed one, you were the goat lying on the turf while some guy galloped for the end zone with traces of your genetic code on his cleats. So Marcus kept his focus on not screwing up, and it went pretty well. There was one lapse in the second quarter that gave up a big gain, but when the receiver was finally brought down, it was Marcus who did the bringing. So that was worth something.

"Nice tackle, Jordan," Coach Barker approved. "Thirty yards too late, but I like the technique."

"Technique?" Troy complained. "That cost us a field goal!"

Barker glared the QB back to the bench, and Marcus kept his mouth shut. No sense upsetting Golden Boy in the middle of a game.

Luckily, the result of this contest was never in much doubt. The Steelers of Central Regional High were no match for the defending champs. Troy's high-powered offense took up just where it had left off with last year's perfect season. Marcus didn't like the guy, but he couldn't claim that Troy wasn't any good. He was efficient, effective, and accurate in his throws. Even more impressive, he projected total control while on the field. It was more than the way he took snaps and made handoffs and threw passes. Something in his body language drew attention like an industrial magnet. It definitely drew Alyssa's attention. Throughout her cheers and chants and routines, her eyes never left him.

It happened in the fourth quarter. The Raiders were

driving yet again, up 28–3. Luke had beaten his man and was all alone in the middle of the field, waving his arms, no one between him and the distant end zone. Instead, Troy opted for a short dump to Ron for a three-yard gain.

Marcus turned to Barker, but the coach seemed to have missed it, probably assuming that Troy simply hadn't noticed Luke so wide open. Marcus knew better. Number Seven had seen Luke all right, but he'd also seen the big defensive end closing in on him at top speed. Troy could have made that play, but he would have been flattened. He'd gotten rid of the ball to avoid the pop.

It was as clear to Marcus as if he'd been inside Troy's helmet. It was the way Marcus had played until recently— running scared. And it meant that even Golden Boy was human. Marcus took some comfort in that. Sure, he'd been banished to the defensive secondary, but he had a slight advantage over Troy Popovich. And he'd picked it up from the guy's own father.

The feeling—a distinctly Charlie-esque desire for contact—was almost tangible as Marcus took the field for the next defensive series. He was going to get out there and pop somebody.

He didn't have long to wait. Down by several scores late in the game, the Steelers' quarterback was throwing deep, looking for a miracle comeback. On third and ten, one of those passes came in Marcus's direction.

He pounded along the sideline, matching the receiver stride for side. When he saw his man glance over his shoulder, he knew the ball was on its way. He risked a quick look of his own. There it was, descending like a cruise missile, a little wobbly but well thrown.

He waited for his opponent to leap first—striking too soon would draw a penalty. Then, the instant the receiver left his feet, Marcus did too. Impact was sudden, jarring, primal—Marcus's shoulder rammed into the Steeler's gut, and more than four hundred pounds of muscle, bone, and equipment slammed together at high speed. The pass hit its target right in the numbers, but the sprawling receiver couldn't make the play. Shaken by the force of his own tackle, Marcus saw the deflected ball out of the corner of his eye. A split second before he crashed to the ground, he was able to get his left hand around it and pull it to his chest.

Interception, Raiders.

"Waste of a good play" was Troy's pronouncement, with a gesture in the direction of the scoreboard.

"Great hit, Jordan!" cheered the coach. "We'll make a corner of you yet!"

The clock ticked down to a Raiders victory. Perfect season number two was under way. There was so much praise blowing around the sidelines that some of it even fell on the lowly cornerback. His high-five meter may not have registered among the titans of the offense, but he was definitely a member of the club.

The bleachers thinned as spectators headed for the exits. Families and friends stopped by the bench to congratulate the players.

Barbara Jordan waved her camera as she made her way to the parking lot. "Got some great shots," she called. "You're going to be in the Sunday paper!"

She meant the team, of course, not him specifically. Probably the winning QB. Breakfast tomorrow wasn't going to go down very well if he had to look at a picture of Troy on page one.

He spied Charlie's tall form behind the bench, above the heads of the crowd, his wife at his side. Mrs. Popovich wrapped her arms around Number Seven's expansive shoulder pads. "You were wonderful, honey."

Troy accepted the hug without embarrassment, but his eyes never left Charlie, who walked purposefully straight past his son. Marcus was struck by a wave of amazement. The King of Pop was coming to *him*.

"Good game, Mac. You never could have done it without me."

Marcus grinned. "Damn right I couldn't."

Troy untangled himself from his mother and took his father's arm. "Come on, Dad. Let's go home."

Mrs. Popovich stepped in. "Charlie, didn't Troy play a fantastic game?"

Charlie nodded vigorously. "Oh, yeah—sure, like always!"

The look Troy gave Marcus could have melted his faceguard.

CHAPTER TEN

The new drill was called Shark Bait.

It was Charlie's most sadistic creation to date. A sickly crabapple tree was used as a catapult to send the punt skyward. The receiver, positioned halfway up the Paper Airplane, had to jump for it, bring in the awkward, spinning ball, and land on the grass below. There, he truly was "shark bait"—exposed, unprotected, unable even to brace himself for impact as the tackler plowed him over.

They had been at it for close to two hours, without a break. As always, Marcus was getting the worst of the exchange, but he fought on, determined to get his licks in.

If he could induce a grunt or a gasp from the NFL's King of Pop, that was a major achievement. As for the pain signals screaming from every cell of his own body, he almost welcomed them. It used to be the *result* of the collision that he wanted—a good tackle or block, an approving smile behind Barker's usual backhanded compliment. Now the hitting was an end in itself. The impact felt good, and the hurt that went with it was something he craved. It had even seeped into his life outside football. He'd be sitting in class, knowing he should be thinking about the lesson or the Vespa's next oil change or the feeling of Alyssa's lips on his, with the promise of more to come if the two of them ever had the chance to be alone together. Instead, he had another kind of body contact in mind. All he wanted to do was tackle a brick wall. Charlie had turned him into a pop addict.

Nothing was harder than catching a football that was twirling end over end. As he dropped from the Paper Airplane, he struggled to pull the ball in while at the same time concentrating on achieving a solid landing with no twisted ankles. As always, Charlie's tackle was textbook. As he wrapped Marcus up, his shoulder slammed the ball free. The momentum of his lunge drove his head right into Marcus's upper arm.

Marcus was aware of an uncoupling deep inside him, as if his skeleton was made of Lego blocks and some basic connection had popped loose. A split second later, he was in unbearable pain.

Not even an NFL tough guy could ignore the cries of agony as his companion writhed on the grass, hugging himself against a level of discomfort that would have been unimaginable just a moment before.

"What is it, Mac? Where'd you get dinged?"

"My shoulder!" Marcus gasped, barely able to summon the breath required for speech. "I think it's broken!"

Charlie looked dubious. "I would have felt that. Probably just a dislocation. Happens all the time."

"Not to me!" Marcus yowled. His shoulder was on fire, the searing waves radiating from his fingertips to the center of his chest.

Charlie grabbed him by the good arm and hauled him to his feet. The head rush nearly caused him to black out.

"Here's what you do," said the NFL veteran, indicating the *Remembrance* sculpture. "You've got to ram your shoulder into that statue as hard as you can."

"Are you crazy?" Marcus howled.

"You've got to be moving fast enough to knock the bone back into the joint. It's going to hurt like hell."

"It hurts like hell already!"

Charlie looked mildly annoyed. "And it'll keep on hurting until you fix it."

It was too much to ask. Never before had Marcus suffered such torment. The prospect of touching a cobweb was unthinkable, much less a block of granite.

"I've got to get to a doctor!"

"He's just going to tell you the same thing," the King of Pop warned.

"He's not going to tell me to run into a statue!"

"No, he'll push it back in for you," Charlie reasoned. "Here, you want me to try?"

Marcus shrank away. "Don't touch me—please! I've got to go to the emergency room. There's no way I can get there on my bike! Have you got a car, Charlie?"

"I'll get it!" Charlie promised. "Just sit tight. I'll be back in ten minutes!" And he sprinted off with long athletic strides.

Marcus was too miserable to notice the fifty-four-year-old's impressive speed. He sat with his back against the Paper Airplane, willing himself to remain absolutely still, because movement was out of the question. The simple act of breathing in and out was all he could manage.

Come on, Charlie. Hurry up.

The pain was so intense that he actually zoned out for a while, although he couldn't be certain if he'd slept or fainted.

"Charlie?" he said groggily.

But he was alone. Not only that—the sun had changed position, and was considerably lower in the sky. He looked down at his watch. Forty minutes had passed! Where was Charlie?

No—no time to think about that. He needed relief from this torment, and he needed it now.

He couldn't walk to the hospital, and he couldn't ride

the Vespa in this condition. He probably couldn't even crawl out of the park to fall at the feet of some random pedestrian. There was only one option left.

He staggered to his feet, biting the side of his mouth to keep from losing consciousness again. He took a few steps back. He'd become much tougher since training with Charlie, but this required reserves of courage even he wasn't sure he possessed.

Holding his breath, he ran forward at full tilt and slammed his shoulder into the solid granite.

He heard himself scream, and that was all he was aware of for several minutes. When he awoke, his lunch was all down the front of his shirt, and the pain was gone. In wonder, he flexed his shoulder, moving his arm up and down. He was fine. A little sore, but only a little. Fine.

Unbelievable! Charlie was right.

Charlie . . .

How could a grown man leave a teenager in such a condition? How could he just walk away like that, promising help and never coming back? Could anybody be so selfish? Did he consider himself so big a sports star that other people simply didn't matter?

I don't care how much he's helped me with football! I'm done with that guy.

He started for the parking lot and his Vespa, still amazed that the terrible agony was so suddenly gone. To be utterly incapacitated and, an instant later, totally back to normal seemed almost like magic. Clearly, it had been no big deal to Charlie. He pictured an NFL locker room, with howling players bodychecking the cinder-block walls to autocorrect their various dislocations.

The bike's motor roared to life, and he tooled out of the main entrance of the park, more shaken by Charlie's behavior than the memory of the blinding pain. This man was supposed to be his *friend*. He had taken Marcus under his wing and generously shared his football experience. He had even greeted Marcus before going up to his own son at the Raiders-Steelers game.

What a jerk!

No sooner had Marcus reached Poplar Street than a shiny black Cadillac SUV crested the rise. A familiar set of broad shoulders was hunched over the wheel. It was Charlie, peering through the windshield with the intense concentration of a chess master pondering a critical move.

Marcus waved his arms. "Hey!"

The big Cadillac roared straight on past.

He didn't see me!

Marcus's brow knit. No, that wasn't quite it. More like Charlie *had* seen him—and had looked right through him.

He twisted the throttle, and the scooter took off in hot pursuit. Putt-putting around town, there weren't a lot of opportunities for the Vespa to show what it could do. Props to Comrade Stalin—it was a great gift, even with the many strings attached. He flashed past the SUV and then ditched the bike in the grass just in time to flag Charlie down from the side of the road.

The passenger window receded into the door frame.

"What happened?" Marcus demanded. "You were supposed to come pick me up!"

Charlie's face was blank. "What?"

"That's not funny, man!" Marcus exploded. "You left me screaming my head off with a dislocated shoulder!"

"What you have to do is find a good, solid tree—"

"It isn't dislocated *now*! I had to fix it myself when you didn't show up to take me to the emergency room!"

Charlie frowned. "Is this some kind of joke?"

"You can't act like you don't know what I'm talking about! It just happened!"

"Mac—"

"You know my real name!" stormed Marcus. "I've told it to you twenty times! I may not have played pro football, but I'm a person too. Where do you get off trying to stiff me for your half of that broken window? You owe me a hundred and fifty-five bucks!"

The former linebacker's eyes narrowed. "Are you trying to rip me off?"

"Forget it." If Charlie wanted to screw a high school kid out of what amounted to pocket change for a guy behind the wheel of a seventy-thousand-dollar SUV, Marcus wasn't going to fight with him. It just reinforced the image of the egotistical pro athlete, so self-centered that he couldn't even devote a few minutes of his day to giving a teenager obviously in agony a lift to the hospital.

He got back on his bike, giving the SUV a wide berth as he made a left turn into traffic. He was burning again, but this time it was with shame. How duped he'd been by this old weirdo! How quick to mistake a few tackling pointers and a glitzy stat sheet for friendship! He felt like an idiot.

The sound of car horns behind him drew his eyes to the mirror. The Cadillac was making a U-turn. Was Charlie chasing him now? Well, if he was, he'd picked the wrong kind of scooter to go up against. A twist of the throttle and soon the Vespa was up to seventy, whizzing by Three Alarm Park, the SUV just a dot in the rearview.

He had already wasted more than enough time on Charlie Popovich.

The collage had once held a place of honor on Troy's bedroom wall. Now it lay at the bottom of his junk drawer, buried under old CD cases and a long-defunct Scooby-Doo puzzle with two pieces missing.

"Troy!" came his mother's voice from downstairs.

He ignored her, scrutinizing his third-grade handwriting on the construction paper: *Number 55 in Action*.

His father's eyes stared back at him from every conceivable angle. The artwork was a patchwork of dozens of football cards from the King of Pop's playing days. Troy made no move to touch it; he never did. But rarely did a day go by when he didn't open the drawer to look at it.

"Troy, get down here!"

"I'm busy," he mumbled, using his pinky finger to slide an arcade token off Charlie's San Diego rookie card.

"Now!"

Mrs. Popovich was at the base of the stairs, practically shaking with anger. He caught an expression of mock sympathy from his sister. Chelsea the spectator—she was enjoying this.

His mother grabbed his wrist and towed him into the kitchen, where French doors led out to the driveway. There sat the black SUV, parked at an odd angle. A large dent marred the front bumper.

"Don't look at me," he defended himself. "I can't afford the gas to take that monster around the corner. You probably got dinged in a parking lot."

"I haven't been in a parking lot," Mrs. Popovich said icily. "The car's been here all day."

"Well, I didn't hit it," said Troy. "Check my Mustang—it's clean."

"He couldn't have hit it," Chelsea put in. "The dent's on the wrong side of the car."

Their mother was exasperated. "Then who—"

A loud, juicy crunch stopped her in her tracks. The three peered through the doorway to the den, where Charlie reclined on the couch in front of the TV, dismantling a pear.

Troy's brow furrowed. "Dad doesn't drive anymore, does he?"

"He took me to the cell phone place," Chelsea supplied.

"Well, okay, if there's someone in the car with him," said Mrs. Popovich. "But alone?"

"Where does he ever go that he can't walk to?" asked Troy.

His mother looked stricken, her lips hardening into a thin line. Wordlessly, she removed the Cadillac key chain from a wall hook and hid it deep inside a kitchen drawer.

CHAPTER ELEVEN

For Marcus, cutting Charlie out of his life was both easy and hard. It was a simple matter to stop heading for Three Alarm Park after football practice every day. But he missed the former linebacker.

How dumb was that? Getting attached to someone who ripped you off, let you take the blame for what *he* did, and walked away when you were on the ground, howling in agony—it didn't make sense. And Marcus had understood from day one that he was dealing with a very peculiar guy. So what was it that he liked about the man? The NFL connection? No, Marcus had known Charlie long before he'd learned about his pro career. The man's larger-than-life personality? His unfailing willingness to play—not just football, but *life*? Maybe—but didn't weirdness trump charm?

That left just the hitting. Marcus missed that most of all. Even the dislocated shoulder hadn't dulled his longing for the crunch of physical contact. The King was gone, and he had taken the pop with him.

The only pop in Marcus's life now came at the Raiders' practice, and it wasn't the same caliber as he'd become accustomed to. Champions or not, no Raider could administer a tackle that had fourteen years of NFL experience behind it. All Marcus could do was throw his own body around with the skill and abandon he had learned from Charlie.

It set Coach Barker's head to full bobble. "Attaway, Jordan! Pay attention, you guys! This is supposed to be a full-speed workout, not a ballet recital!"

From the ranks of the cheerleaders, Alyssa added her expert judgment. "You don't hit like any quarterback I've ever seen."

"Maybe that's why I get fewer snaps every practice," Marcus complained.

His physical play impressed the coach so much that, in the Raiders' second game, his duties were increased to include offense. Not quarterback, of course—that was still Troy. Now he was a fullback, never to touch the ball, but to block for Ron.

To his surprise, he was good at it. High school linebackers turned out to be much softer targets than the rock-solid King of Pop. Ron had his best game ever as a rusher, which induced Barker to keep the ball on the ground, much to the consternation of Troy. It filled Marcus with a mammoth sense of accomplishment. If he couldn't play quarterback, the next best thing was to make the experience less pleasant for Golden Boy.

Troy was shaken by the change in strategy. Perhaps it was the endless handoffs that took him out of his usual confident rhythm. When he did throw a pass, he seemed hurried in the face of even the slightest defensive pressure. Coach Barker didn't seem to notice any of this. To him, offense was offense, and it made no difference if the yardage came from Troy's arm or Ron's legs. The Raiders were winning handily, and the second perfect season was moving forward right on schedule. Alyssa, however, scrutinized her ex from the apex of the cheerleaders' pyramid. And while her exterior may have been pure supermodel, deep down she had the soul of Vince Lombardi. She knew something was up.

Marcus was surprised at how unsettled he was by Charlie's presence in the bleachers. The former linebacker had really gotten under his skin. In spite of everything that had happened, the guy had brought out a dimension of Marcus Jordan, Football Player, that he'd never even known was there.

Troy got right in his face on the sidelines. "What are you doing, Jordan?"

"You're steaming my visor," Marcus growled, refusing to be intimidated.

"You think I'm blind?" Troy demanded. "You've been staring up at my old man the whole game. What's he to you?"

"If he didn't tell you, why should I?" Marcus shot back, a little chagrined that his glances at the bleachers were so obvious.

"This is your last warning—get his autograph and back off!" He gave Marcus a heavy shove, sending him stumbling backward into a group of teammates.

Barker was there in a heartbeat. "You—Jordan. Hit the showers."

"Me?" Marcus was indignant.

The coach's head bobbed menacingly. *"Now."*

Marcus's blood boiled all the way to the locker-room hut. He had blocked like a lion and played steadfast defense, while Troy had been adequate at best.

He was just kicking out of his cleats when the shaking of pom-poms signaled a new arrival. Alyssa.

"There are still a couple of minutes on the clock," he told her irritably.

"Twenty-point lead. No cheers required." She sat down beside him on the bench, resetting the short skirt of her uniform. Her confidence was infinite. It might have been a men's changing room, but Alyssa was welcome everywhere . . . because she was Alyssa. "Good game today."

"Yeah, I'm sure Ron will tell his grandchildren about this one."

She smiled appreciatively. "People notice blocking. And defense. And nice buns—things like that."

"What about gun-shy quarterbacks?" he asked.

She thought it over. "Maybe, maybe not. Either way, coming off thirteen straight wins, you get the benefit of the doubt for a few weeks."

He tossed a wadded-up sock into his open locker. "In other words, it's all my fault."

"You're pissed. I understand. But there are ways of making you unpissed." She leaned over and kissed him. "You're coming to the party tonight, right?"

"What party?"

"At Luke's. His parents are away for the weekend."

He made a face. "My invitation must have been lost in the mail."

She shrugged. "You're on the team."

Marcus was unconvinced. He had worked hard to make a contribution to the Raiders, and most of the players acknowledged it. But there was only one player who really counted.

"It doesn't matter anyway," she persisted, "because you also happen to be a personal friend of *mine*. And," she said, sweetening the deal, "I know every nook and cranny of that house."

He took a deep breath. "What time?"

■ ■ ■

Luke Derrigan lived in Seneca Hill, the older, richer part of town. In contrast with the gated communities of McMansions on fake waterways near the outlet mall, this was a neighborhood of stately homes about a quarter mile from downtown.

The house was lit up like Las Vegas, and the gut-level pounding of hip-hop bass rustled the tree branches, even though doors and windows were tightly closed for noise control.

Marcus was stowing the Vespa by a hedge when there was a sharp "Ow!" He looked down to find Ron intertwined with one of the cheerleaders—Katie or Kelli, something like that—under cover of the hedge.

"Beat it—" Ron began before his night vision took in the newcomer. "Marcus! How's it going, dude? I—didn't think you could make it."

Marcus peered down at his halfback with a cockeyed smile. "Is that why you're in the bushes, Ron? You're the advance guard?"

Katie/Kelli wriggled out of Ron's shadow and favored Marcus with a lipstick-smeared smile. "Great game today. Monster blocking."

"Thanks." It seemed the Raiders had the most knowledgeable cheerleaders in high school football. Alyssa's savvy trickled down the pyramid.

Katie/Kelli's make-out partner seemed uneasy. "Does—uh—*everybody* know you're coming?"

Of all his teammates, Marcus liked Ron best—which

may or may not have explained why he was getting so much enjoyment from watching the guy squirm. "Define 'everybody.'"

Ron flushed. "Don't play dumb. Does Troy know you're crashing?"

"Who says he's crashing?" Katie/Kelli jumped in.

"Hey, I'm down with him being here," Ron said quickly. "But be smart, okay? Troy's going to pull up, and the first thing he'll see is your dorkmobile parked on the front lawn."

"Did Troy blow open those big holes for you today?" Marcus demanded.

"That's why I'm looking out for you, man. I'm not saying go home, but keep a low profile. And whatever you do, stay away from Alyssa."

Katie/Kellie snorted a laugh. "Like that's going to happen."

Ron made a last-ditch effort. "Just remember—the good of the team."

Right. On one side of the scale was the greater glory of Troy and the Raiders. On the other was Alyssa Fontaine. It wasn't much of a contest. "I'll ditch the bike around the side of the house," he offered.

As Marcus walked the Vespa along the hedge, the front door was thrown open to reveal Calvin Applegate, a golf club cocked high over his head. Marcus ducked just as the flanker swung. With a *splat*, the three-wood vaporized a nectarine that sat on the welcome mat, spraying fruit sludge all over the yard. A crowd of admirers mobbed Calvin, high-fiving raucously.

Marcus stashed the bike and slipped inside. He'd been to football parties back in Kansas, but as a JV player, he'd never been exposed to the full spectrum of mayhem. The air was heavy with beer and sweat, and the floor lurched with the pounding music. Every square foot was crammed with kids, and most seemed to be doing something stupid, if not illegal. The living room was so packed that the dance move of the night was restricted to a vertical hop.

When Luke spied Marcus, he began shouting and gesturing, but he was trapped by bouncing bodies, unable to move or to communicate over the music. Marcus waved blithely back and slipped quickly out of view. Now to find Alyssa before anyone else found him. She was definitely the only thing standing between him and ejection from the party.

A packed house wasn't the easiest place to conduct a search. Every step of progress had to be bulldozed. It took fifteen minutes to get to the den, only to end up stuck in a cheering crowd watching two idiots playing air hockey with their noses.

Like most good receivers, Luke had large, strong hands. They clamped onto Marcus's shoulders with some power.

"Who told you to come here, Jordan?"

Marcus played dumb. "Great party, man! Love the house!"

Luke took a deep breath. "Listen—"

There was a great crash as one of the nose pucksters climbed onto the air hockey table, his weight snapping one of the legs. He tumbled into the spectators, setting off a domino effect of falling partygoers.

"Hey! *Hey!*" Luke rushed to the scene and was absorbed into the writhing mass of upended humanity. Marcus took advantage of the opportunity to escape down the basement stairs, picking his way around the guests who had settled there in search of free space.

The basement was less crowded but wilder. Bodies were suspended from pipes in the ceiling—some kind of bar-hanging competition. A Frisbee game was in progress using a Dora the Explorer toddler toilet seat. Someone was trying to machine wash a leather beanbag chair, and the washer screeched in protest, spewing suds all over the laundry room. The tennis-racket air guitar contest was morphing into a tennis-racket light saber battle. A bunch of Good Samaritans had gotten the idea to plug up a hole in the wall with chewing gum. When the Derrigans returned from their weekend away, they were definitely going to have a few choice words for their son. Or maybe a trashed house was a small price to pay for another perfect season. That was the only thing that seemed to matter in Kennesaw, Gateway to the Gunks.

Marcus ducked to avoid the airborne seat and stepped between air guitarists. He was grabbed from behind, and for an instant, he thought Luke had caught up with him again. But no—the hands were smaller, the grip playful.

He spun around to face Alyssa. "I might be kicked out any minute."

She pressed a finger to his lips and led him through the turbulent laundry room to an unpainted door. The odor was strong but pleasant—a cedar closet. In the darkness, he could make out racks of suits and winter coats.

"Ever been to a party, Marcus? Do you know what they're *for*?"

He was too cowed to answer.

"This." She kissed him, pulling him down onto a pile of sleeping bags and camping blankets.

He had never been a big fan of the move to Kennesaw, but he wasn't complaining now. It was as if all the bad things that had ever happened to him were suddenly lighter than air. No, that wasn't right. The problems were still there; in some cases, they were very close. But they couldn't touch him here. Or maybe it was just that he didn't care about anything outside the confines of the cedar closet. This tiny room was the only universe that mattered, a place where E didn't have to equal mc^2, and none of the other rules applied.

He was so in the moment that when the closet door was thrown open, the sudden blast of light nearly stopped his heart. Shocked, Marcus and Alyssa jumped apart, blinking, struggling to reorient themselves. It was like being yanked from an isolation tank and tossed into a bathtub filled with ice water.

At last—focus. Troy, silhouetted in the doorway. His fist lashed out, catching Marcus on the chin. Marcus barely flinched. After all, he had taken incoming fire from the Popovich who had refined it to the level of high art. He threw himself at the Raiders' captain, spearing his shoulder into Troy's solar plexus, sending the two of them rolling in the suds on the laundry-room floor.

A big lineman—Gary Somebody—yanked Marcus up and held him from behind.

Alyssa got in her ex's face. "*I* told him to come tonight! If you want to be pissed at someone, try me!"

"I *am* pissed at you!" Troy yelled at her.

"Then leave Marcus alone! This isn't his fault!"

"Hey!" Marcus said sharply. "I'm not afraid of him!" He shook himself free of Gary and spread his arms, presenting his unprotected body. "Be my guest, bust me one. I can take it. The question is, can *you*?"

"What are you talking about?" Troy's voice was as cold as liquid nitrogen.

"Like you don't know."

"Coming here was a mistake, dead man."

"You don't own this house!" shouted Alyssa. "And you definitely don't own me! You don't even want to!"

The quarterback's anger morphed into a pained expression. "Maybe it's not like that."

"You tell me, then—what *is* it like?"

"Hey!" Luke was in the process of unplugging the washing machine in an attempt to stem the tide of suds.

"Let's all chill out. It's supposed to be a party."

Troy returned his furious attention to Marcus. "And he's crashing!"

Luke refused to be intimidated. "He's got a playbook, he's got a jersey. He's one of us. It doesn't help the team if you guys fight."

"Where was he when we were making history last year?" Troy demanded. "Coach says we have to take him, so we take him. But he's not one of us."

Troy panned the crowd, looking for the familiar backup he'd always been afforded as their quarterback and leader. The faces were expressionless—not hostile, but not supportive either. Certainly, no one was hustling Marcus upstairs and out the front door.

Ron reached into the dryer and pulled a can of beer out of the ice. "Heads!" He tossed it to Marcus.

Marcus caught it and popped the top. He didn't even like beer, but this was a symbolic moment. You didn't turn a thing like that down.

"Troy!" called Ron. And the next can was flipped to the quarterback. Troy caught it, but he didn't look happy.

At that moment, the lights flickered as the pounding music upstairs died abruptly. There was an urgent shouted exchange, and then a girl's voice rasped, *"Troy!"*

"Chelsea?" Troy looked around. "Go home. This isn't your—"

He fell silent at the sight of her on the landing. Her face was bright red.

She ran to her brother, nearly slipping on the wet floor, and began whispering in his ear.

Marcus was on his way back to Alyssa when he overheard Troy hiss, "What do you mean, missing?"

"You mean Charlie?" he blurted.

Not even the punch from a few minutes before could have prepared him for the explosiveness of Troy's reaction. The quarterback lunged at him, shoving him back with such violence that he might have gone through the drywall if Gary hadn't been there to catch him.

"This is none of your business!" Troy roared. "You're lucky to be alive, man!"

Marcus was blown away. Sure, he knew that Charlie's kids were protective of their celebrity dad, but this was different. Chelsea was genuinely terrified, and Troy was clearly rattled by something beyond finding his ex-girlfriend in a cedar closet with Marcus. Why? Charlie had been at the game that afternoon, so his "disappearance" couldn't have been longer than a few hours. He'd been absent from his family for at least that long—training with Marcus in the park—countless times. Why was everyone so freaked out about it now?

The rush of sudden understanding came with the sense that he should have known all along. There was no new information, just dots he'd never bothered to connect before. Yes, the man was odd and quirky, but there was more to it than that. Something was wrong with Charlie. Something serious.

"Sorry, guys," Troy mumbled. "I've got to go take care of something."

Brother and sister started upstairs.

Marcus started after them. "I'm coming with you!"

Troy spun around, eyes wide with rage.

"I might be able to help," Marcus persisted.

Ron stopped him with a stiff arm, gentle but firm. "Back off, man. It's a family thing."

Alyssa touched the center of his chest, tracing contrite circles with her index finger. "Sorry, Marcus. I didn't think it would turn out like this."

"It's fine," he mumbled.

It *wasn't* fine. The mood was gone, and not even a beautiful cheerleader—one who actually understood the sport she was cheering about—could bring it back again.

Besides, Charlie was missing. And Marcus had a pretty good idea where the former linebacker might be.

CHAPTER TWELVE

Marcus had never been to Three Alarm Park at night. It was deserted, but that wasn't unusual. The place could be just as empty at high noon. What he hadn't expected was how dark it was, with no lights at all beyond the parking lot.

He got off the Vespa and ventured through the public gardens. By the time he'd reached the playing field, he was squinting into the shadows. He cupped his hands to his mouth. *"Charlie!"* he shouted into the gloom. *"Hey, Charlie!"*

"Who's there?" came a call from the distance.

"It's me—Marcus."

"Mac?" Definitely Charlie. "Is that you?"

The voice seemed to be coming from above.

His gaze gradually focused on a murky form, tall and angular, atop the Paper Airplane. Of course. He should've known that Charlie would be lurking where he felt most comfortable—twenty feet up.

He began to climb, negotiating the steep incline using a combination of memory and blind faith. As Marcus's ascent progressed, Charlie came into shadowy relief, perched near the sculpture's summit, for all the world like he was relaxing on a lazy afternoon and not the subject of a frenzied late-night manhunt. "What are you doing, Charlie? Why are you sitting here in the pitch black?"

"What took you so long?" the former linebacker demanded. "Where's the ball?"

Marcus was thunderstruck. "It's the middle of the night! People are searching for you!"

Charlie looked nervous. "You talked to my dad?"

His *dad*? Marcus frowned, and then posed the question he had never asked before yet suddenly seemed very relevant. "How old are you, Charlie?"

"Bite me," Charlie replied in annoyance. "Like you don't know."

"Seriously—I forget."

The King of Pop snorted. "Three weeks younger than you. Quit fooling around, Mac."

Marcus let out a tremulous breath. How many nights had he spent wondering why a retired NFL vet had nothing better to do with his time than play football with a teenager. The answer? For some reason, he thought he was a teenager, too.

How was that possible? Charlie knew he'd had an entire pro sports career, didn't he? Come to think of it, Marcus had been the one who'd mentioned the NFL, not Charlie. And while the guy never denied having a wife and children, he never talked about them.

How can he believe he's my age when he knows he's got two kids who are my age?

Or *did* he know?

"Chelsea and Troy are worried about you," Marcus ventured carefully. When there was no reply, he added, "You know who they are, right?"

"Course I do," Charlie muttered almost belligerently.

Marcus didn't dare push it. He wasn't sure how much he should try to reason with Charlie, who was obviously confused. Whatever was wrong with the guy, it was a job for a doctor or a shrink, not a second-string quarterback. The important thing was to get the man back to his anxious family.

"Why don't you let me give you a ride home?"

"Yeah, I guess it's time to call it a night."

Squeezing two football players onto the Vespa's small seat took some engineering.

"When did you get this thing, Mac?" Charlie asked, impressed. "You been holding out on me?"

"Just hang on," Marcus advised. He picked up his

helmet and, after a moment's deliberation, set it into place on his passenger's head. He wasn't even certain he'd be welcomed by the Popovich family when he returned their missing person to them. The last thing he wanted to do was risk the package being damaged in transit.

He started the bike's motor and turned left out of the park onto Poplar Street, the direction Charlie usually headed after their training sessions.

All at once, Charlie emitted a roar of mirth, waving and pointing.

Marcus struggled to keep the scooter in balance despite the shifting weight. "What's so funny?"

"Looks like Old Man Dingley finally got what's coming to him!"

"Who's Dingley?" Then he remembered. It was the name Charlie had once called Kenneth Oliver. He gazed at the exterminator's shop.

The storefront had been completely plastered with toilet paper, and loose streamers of tissue were fluttering in the breeze.

Marcus was wide-eyed. "Did you do that, Charlie?"

"Wish I had," the former linebacker replied heartily. "We should find whoever did it and shake his hand."

Marcus noticed the shreds of toilet paper sticking out of Charlie's sleeves. The hand the old guy wanted to shake was his own. Why would he lie about it to Marcus, of all people—his co-conspirator in the sugaring?

He sighed. "Okay, where to?"

"Oh—you know."

"No, I don't," Marcus said seriously. "Where do you live?"

"It's just up the road."

"Up what road?" Marcus persisted. "Poplar Street?"

"You can't miss it."

Marcus twisted on the bike to regard his passenger. The former linebacker looked uncomfortable and completely lost at sea.

"Hey." Eyes narrowed, Marcus gestured toward the TP'd K.O Pest Control. "Remember when we sugared that place?"

Charlie's blank face was suddenly alight with diabolical excitement. "That's a great idea! It'll serve him right after all the times he's been on our case."

It was exactly the response Marcus was expecting, yet it was jarring nonetheless. Charlie didn't remember the elaborate planning and execution of Bug Day. He had already forgotten TP'ing the shop, which must have taken place in the past few hours. He couldn't even seem to explain where he lived.

Marcus rode back up Seneca Hill, figuring that if all else failed, he could return to Luke's party. Surely somebody there knew where Troy's house was. It wasn't his first choice, though. Troy and Chelsea's whispered powwow in Luke's basement and their hostility toward anybody who nosed around their father added up to one inescapable conclusion: Charlie's problem was strictly hush-hush.

Marcus kept his eyes on the mirrors to better decode what Charlie meant by muttered orders like "Turn here!" and "This way!" He was pretty sure they were wandering in circles.

Charlie's mumbled monologue didn't exactly inspire confidence. "Whose stupid idea was it to make every single house look exactly the same? What a way to run a town— *Watch out!*"

There was a terrified bark, and Marcus swerved to avoid a collision with a light-haired dog. The animal bounded over to Charlie.

"How's it going, Boomer? You miss me?"

"Daddy!" Chelsea exploded out the front door. Without acknowledging Marcus on the Vespa, she took her father's hand and led him to the house. "Everyone was so worried!"

Charlie was mystified. "What for? Where do I ever go? Down, boy," he added to the dog, who was clawing at his pant leg.

"Silky's a girl," Chelsea reminded him quietly.

Mrs. Popovich met them at the door. She hugged her husband and told her daughter, "Call Troy on his cell and let him know everything's okay." She noticed Marcus parked at the curb and waved.

"If it happens again, try Three Alarm Park," Marcus advised.

"Thanks for bringing him home," she called, her voice catching.

Those were the first civil words Marcus had ever heard from a member of the Popovich family.

Two A.M. found Marcus in the kitchen, pounding the keyboard of the computer. Despite the exhaustion of a long and wild night, sleep was eluding him. He couldn't relax—not until he'd solved the puzzle.

He scoured the internet, using keywords like *forgetfulness, confusion,* and *memory loss,* but those always seemed to lead him to sites selling vitamin supplements, "miracle drugs," and subscriptions to health magazines. On www.wellnessweb.usa, his search parameters led him to the subtopic *Senility,* but that couldn't be right. Old people went senile; Charlie was only fifty-four.

He tried different combinations of his keywords on the WellnessWeb site, generating articles on everything from mental illness to hypertension to drug addiction to amnesia. The problem was that his search parameters were too general. Millions of people were confused or forgetful, probably for millions of different reasons. What he needed was something specific to Charlie.

Beside *memory loss* he typed three letters: *NFL.*

The link that appeared led to an article in the *North American Journal of Medicine*:

NEW DATA TIES CONCUSSIONS TO ALZHEIMER'S

The NFL is studying a report suggesting that athletes who suffer multiple concussions are at increased risk of developing early-onset Alzheimer's disease. Recent findings indicate that repeated head trauma injuries, common in high-contact sports such as football and boxing, can cause permanent neurological damage, resulting in a gradual and irreversible decline in short-term memory, language skills, perception of space and time, and eventually the ability to care for oneself.

While Alzheimer's is ordinarily associated with the elderly, the rare early-onset form of the disease has been known to affect patients as young as thirty. The investigation of a link to sports injuries began after the autopsy of Philadelphia defensive back Andre Waters showed signs of the disorder. Concussions have long been suspected in the Alzheimer's cases of NFL veterans Ralph Wenzel, John Mackey, and Ted Johnson. . . .

The piece went on to describe a condition that destroys memory in an oddly selective way. A patient might forget what he had for breakfast ten minutes earlier, but retain clear recollections from decades before. The effect was that many Alzheimer's sufferers appeared to be living in the past.

Like a retired athlete who thinks he's a teenager.

It explained everything about Charlie's confusion and odd behavior. No wonder Chelsea and Troy were so touchy about their father. They were trying to keep his condition a secret. That's why Mrs. Popovich made regular visits to all her husband's usual haunts around town to pay his tabs. As a local hero, Charlie was cut a lot of slack, so long as the stores got their money eventually. Because he was a larger-than-life character around Kennesaw, people assumed he was just idiosyncratic, colorful, quirky. No one realized how sick he was.

Yet.

Marcus was aware of a lump in his throat the size of a cannonball. According to wellnessweb.usa, Alzheimer's disease never got better. Right now, Charlie had enough memory and mental capacity to function within the small, protected universe he had carved for himself. But that wouldn't last forever. The article said the deterioration might be slow, but it would be relentless. Eventually, poor Charlie's mind would be wiped practically clean.

What then?

On Sunday, Marcus was at the desk in his room, gazing blearily at the Raiders' playbook and struggling to keep his eyes open, when he was startled by a sudden clatter at the window. As he went to investigate, a handful of gravel machine-gunned against the glass.

He looked beyond it at the Volvo wagon parked at the curb. He didn't recognize the car, but the girl loading up another handful of rocks was perfectly familiar. Alyssa.

He opened the window and called down, "We have a doorbell."

She smiled up at him. "Sorry."

She wasn't sorry. She didn't have to be. Her get-out-of-jail-free card had no limitations and no blackout dates. *Must be nice,* thought Marcus. He went downstairs and let her in.

"I thought your mom might be home or something," she explained. "I'm not sure how much she knows about me."

"She's out in the Gunks, shooting." He added, "Pictures, not deer."

Alyssa beamed. "Works for me either way." She threw her arms around his neck and pressed her lips to his.

He didn't push her away, but he didn't kiss her back, either.

She retreated a step. "You're mad."

"I'm not," he replied honestly. "That's the problem. I should be chewing rusty nails after last night. What would have happened if I couldn't throw a good block? Would you still visit me in intensive care?"

She was unrepentant. "Don't I get points for being right? I told you they'd come around."

"It damn near didn't go that way. What if Ron hadn't been there? Or if Gary hadn't let go? Or if Luke didn't mind bloodstains on his laundry-room floor? What if Chelsea hadn't stormed the basement in time to distract the psycho-in-chief?"

"We didn't do anything wrong," she insisted. "You had every right to be there—as a Raider and as my date."

"Being right doesn't unfracture your skull," Marcus reminded her. "At a certain point you have to forget about what's right and do what makes sense. Face it—you and me makes no sense."

"It made sense last night," she protested, "until we got ambushed."

"I'm not going to pretend I'm not into you," Marcus said. "But what does *that* mean? How many guys aren't?"

"I don't want those guys; I want you."

"This whole town sees you as Troy's," Marcus told her. "And there's a part of you that still sees yourself the same way."

"That's great news for me. You can find another girlfriend, but I belong to Troy till the end of time. Maybe we should try fixing him up. Would I be off the hook then?"

He grinned appreciatively. "I only know one other girl in town, and she's his sister."

"This sucks," she pronounced dejectedly. "Couldn't we just—I don't know—hate each other and still fool around?"

"We don't hate each other. We're friends."

"With benefits?" she probed.

The staccato *blurp* of a police siren drew their attention outside. The cruiser pulled up to the curb, flashers on intermittent.

Alyssa pointed. "Isn't that the cop who busted you last time?"

Marcus had a vision of cascades of toilet paper draped over the metal cockroach, filling the doorway of K.O. Pest

Control. He knew then that a lousy weekend was about to get worse.

Officer Deluca peered over his desk. "You know, Marcus, we could take a drive over to the county lockup and see about six hundred innocent men just like you."

"I *am* innocent," Marcus said stubbornly.

"Never said you weren't," the policeman agreed. "But if you don't give me the name of the person who's guilty, this time you're going to get due process, just like I warned you."

"That's not fair!" Marcus exclaimed hotly. "I don't know who did it, so that means it must have been me?"

"You *do* know who did it. Why would you cover for somebody who lets you take the rap?"

"Why would you call out the SWAT team over toilet paper?" Marcus countered.

"It isn't the toilet paper," the officer explained. "It's the pattern of harassment. Mr. Oliver wants to press charges, which is his right as a citizen. It's not going to have a happy ending—not unless you tell me what you know."

It should have been easy. Marcus wasn't familiar with the laws surrounding Alzheimer's, but Charlie probably wasn't even responsible for his actions.

On the other hand, how could Marcus rat out a sick man? The family seemed obsessed with keeping a lid on the King of Pop's condition. A court case would blow that up in their faces. Not that he particularly cared about the delicate sensibilities of Troy and his nasty sister. But there was Charlie to think about, too. The poor guy was on the precipice of a terrible deterioration. He had the right to hold on to his dignity—even if he would ultimately end up at the point where dignity wouldn't mean much to him anymore.

Marcus kept his mouth shut.

Deluca sighed heavily. "Suit yourself." And he began reading Marcus his rights.

This time Mom was decidedly not cool about it. Her photo shoot had taken her deep into the mountains. Ninety feet up a cliff, her cell phone somehow managed to find a signal. There, surrounded by rocky peaks and glacial erratics, Barbara Jordan listened to Officer Deluca's message that she was urgently needed in town to get her son out of a holding cell.

When she finally arrived at the station, she was nearly hysterical. "You've been booked, Marcus. *Booked!* That's on your record now! Who are you covering for? Is it that girl?"

"What girl?" Marcus said bitterly. "That was never going to work."

"Why?" she demanded, the trail dust swirling around her hiking gear. "Why are you so determined not to have a normal life here?"

"Well, for starters," he shot back, "because every time I start to, I get arrested!"

Officer Deluca appeared with a steaming mug of coffee and a stale-looking donut from the staff kitchen. "Sorry it isn't fresher," he said apologetically.

Mrs. Jordan was distraught. "You've been great, Officer. I'm so sorry about all this. I *guarantee* this isn't how Marcus normally behaves."

"Work on him," the cop advised. "The worst part of this is that it's unnecessary. There's no serial killer here. But the longer he clams up, the deeper the hole he digs for himself."

Nor did the grilling end when Marcus and his mother left the station and got into her pickup truck.

"All right, Marcus, you've got to meet me halfway. Do you think I want to be a character in a sitcom, nagging you because 'what will the neighbors say'? Do you think I want to be a drill sergeant like your father—God, just the thought of telling him this turns my blood cold."

"*I'll* tell him." He didn't feel guilty for any of it. But nobody should have to face off with Comrade Stalin over *his* problem—least of all Mom, who'd already endured enough of the good comrade to last a lifetime.

"You—right. You won't even return his phone calls."

"I'll call this time," Marcus promised. "I'll explain everything."

"Then explain it to *me!*"

But he couldn't. He couldn't even explain *why* he couldn't. His silence upset her more than anything. They were a team—only child, single mom—cosurvivors of the Stalinist reign. He had always been completely honest with her. Yet now, with his future potentially on the line, he just couldn't open up.

By the end of the tirade, he was seated in her outer office at the *Advocate*, while she uploaded the shots from her interrupted trip to the Gunks. As if he were eight. She didn't even trust him enough to leave him at home on his own.

He slumped in a visitor's chair, trying not to listen as his mother plowed through the yellow pages, using her cell phone to call lawyers who specialized in juvenile cases. To make matters worse, the newsroom was decorated with dusty black-and-white photographs of the town of Kennesaw over the decades. His chair was directly opposite a picture of the legendary chili cook-off that had given Three Alarm Park its name. The place looked exactly the same, except there had been no Paper Airplane back then—and the trees were smaller, so there was a clearer view of the buildings across the street.

From force of habit, Marcus scowled in the direction of K.O. Pest Control, but the metal cockroach wasn't there. It was the same row of shops, but the sign was different. He squinted to make it out:

DINGLEY'S HARDWARE EMPORIUM

Dingley—that was the name Charlie called Kenneth Oliver. It wasn't just a misfire of a confused mind. It came from something real. There was even a man in the store window, scowling out at the festivities in the park. Old Man Dingley? It was easy to see how Charlie might confuse this guy with Kenneth Oliver. The two didn't look much alike, but they shared the same sour face and aggrieved expression.

The photograph was dated 1971. Charlie would have been sixteen or seventeen at that time.

He sees me in the park, and I become his frame of reference. He relates everything to his memories of himself around my age—Charlie and "Mac," playing football in the park. . . .

He was suddenly struck by an odd thought, something that had never occurred to him before this minute: He'd always assumed that *Mac* was a name you'd call anyone, like *pal* or *buddy*. But if Dingley's Hardware Emporium was real, and Old Man Dingley was real, maybe Mac was real, too.

CHAPTER THIRTEEN

On Monday morning, Marcus arrived at school to see a slender, athletic brunette slipping a note through the vent of his locker door.

What was Alyssa doing? Was it so obvious that he wouldn't have the willpower to stay away from her? And even if this note was totally innocent, Golden Boy might see her planting it—or someone who reported to him might see, and that was practically everybody.

So much for "just friends."

He walked up behind her, reached around, and pulled her baseball cap down over her eyes.

"Guess who."

There was a sharp cry of shock, and a bony elbow slammed into his gut. "Get away!"

Chelsea Popovich.

"Sorry!" he wheezed, rendered breathless by the shot in the stomach and the realization that Chelsea filled out a pair of jeans well enough to be mistaken for Alyssa.

"I left you a note," she said, studying her sneakers. Suddenly, her imploring eyes were gazing up at his. "How come you knew where to find my father when his own family didn't?"

Marcus hesitated, then told her how Charlie had crashed his solitary training sessions at Three Alarm Park, and how the two had begun to practice together. He'd done nothing wrong, yet for some reason it felt like a confession, a deep, dark secret. "It's Alzheimer's, right? Like the other NFL vets I read about?"

Chelsea looked shocked. The family had worked so hard to keep this a secret. They had probably imagined the moment the truth would come out, dreading it.

"I promise I won't spread it all over town," he added.

Her nostrils flared in anger. "We're not *ashamed* of him! It's just nobody's business—including yours."

Marcus nodded. "If he was my dad, I'd be busting with pride. I came to Kennesaw thinking I had football all figured out, but now it seems like everything I know about the game comes from these last few weeks of working with Charlie."

Her cheeks flushed. "Then you're an idiot. You can't

wait for the chance to knock your head until you've got no more brain cells left than my poor father!"

"I don't see Troy quitting," Marcus pointed out.

"Yeah," she snorted. "And there's my mom every week, cheering on her firstborn while he plays Russian roulette with his own skull. No—worse. In Russian roulette, at least you know right away when you've lost. You don't plant these tiny time bombs that go off over twenty-five years. So the next time you're basking in the worship of the crowd, don't expect to see me out there."

Who could blame her for being upset? "I understand," he said gently.

"Please. You figured out what's wrong with Daddy. You learned from him. Maybe you even like him. But there's no way you can understand *this*."

For the first time, it occurred to Marcus that Charlie wasn't the only victim. It had to be just as hard on his family, maybe even harder.

"Well, anyway, sorry about the hat. I thought you were someone else."

"Yeah, I've got a pretty good idea who," she told him.

"What have you got against Alyssa?"

She made a face. "I've already taken up too much of your time."

"I'm not in a hurry."

"She's trouble," said Chelsea. "For Troy or anybody else. Just my opinion."

"So what do you care if I suffer?" Marcus asked, amused.

"You've already made it pretty clear what you think of me."

She looked away. "Maybe I was wrong. First impressions and all that. Thanks for bringing my dad home."

He shrugged. "It was easy. I knew exactly where to look."

"It isn't about easy or hard. It's about caring enough to do it. Do you think your girlfriend cares about anything beyond getting her jollies?"

"She cares about football," Marcus pointed out.

"Wow—sainthood is right around the corner."

"Stop worrying," Marcus assured her. "She's not even my girlfriend."

Chelsea scowled at him. "Who said I was worried?"

Coach Barker reclined in his chair, causing his big head to bobble backward and forward. "I'm loving your effort, Jordan. You put a body on a man as good as any kid I've ever coached. Gain thirty pounds and I could just about guarantee you a four-year scholarship at linebacker."

"I've been working really hard to earn my shot at quarter—"

"This isn't about you," Barker interrupted sharply. "I want to talk about Popovich. You notice anything about his game lately? Anything *different*?"

Yeah—he's afraid to get hit. Maybe Chelsea thinks he's playing Russian roulette, but he's got himself packed in Bubble Wrap!

He kept his mouth shut. You didn't bad-mouth a

teammate to the coach. Not even Troy.

Aloud, he said, "Not sure what you mean, Coach."

"He's not himself," Barker explained. "It's like he's lost his guts. When you get under center, you don't think about what can go wrong. You think about the next big play, and you believe it's going to happen just right, as sure as the earth's going to keep on turning. Once that confidence goes, you're finished at quarterback. You know what I'm talking about? Sure you do."

Marcus nodded excitedly. Winning the starting spot was going to taste twice as sweet because of who he was taking it from.

"And we both know why all this is happening, don't we?" Barker pressed on.

That sour note brought a frown to Marcus's lips. *Does Barker suspect that Troy's gone weak because he's afraid that what happened to his father might happen to him? Does the coach know about Charlie?*

The bobblehead tilted forward and fixed its eyes on Marcus. "It's no secret that you two aren't exactly best friends. You've been after his job, and that's extra pressure. Then there's that Alyssa Fontaine. Don't look so innocent. You think I'm blind?"

Marcus was taken aback. "It's just that—no offense, Coach, but—you've got no business messing with your players' personal lives."

"Wouldn't dream of it. Now find some other skirt to chase, will you?"

Marcus's eyes widened.

"You're the new guy," Barker explained reasonably. "Popovich led this team to a perfect season, and he's my man until he proves he isn't. This is a town where the head cheerleader designs zone blitzes in her sleep. We take our football seriously. Trust me, your love life is not a topic that keeps me up nights—*until* it affects my team."

Marcus left the office astounded by the twisted brilliance of Barker's logic. The guy could justify human sacrifice if it would help him win football games.

Calm down, he reminded himself. *You were trying to cool it with Alyssa anyway. This is just an extra reason to make it stick.*

Still, it rankled him—the thought that Barker would order it.

The athletic department was headquartered between the gym and the pool. The hallways were lined with trophy cases, celebrating past DNA glories, not just in football, but also basketball, soccer, volleyball, swimming, and track.

Marcus's eyes were immediately drawn to a brass plaque that read:

CHARLES POPOVICH
CLASS OF 1973
Third-Round Pick—San Diego Chargers
1977 National Football League Draft
"Our First NFLer, but Not Our Last"

There were no similar plaques, so he had to assume that Charlie really *was* their last—or at least the only one so far. He located the 1973 team picture. There was Charlie, tall and young in the back row, grinning like a winner.

But Charlie wasn't the one Marcus was looking for. He could not shake the feeling that the mysterious Mac might have been on this team, too. A teenage friend you played football with was usually a high school buddy.

Of course, the faces meant nothing to him. But the roster was listed below the photo.

No one was named Mac. But—his eyes homed in on a thick-necked young man to Charlie's left. Name: James McTavish.

McTavish. Mac?

The hearing date was set—December 2. On that day, Marcus was to stand before a judge and explain his involvement as a conspirator in the TP'ing of K.O. Pest Control. If he chose to plead innocent, he would be expected to reveal the name of the guilty party.

"Otherwise," his attorney explained, "I can't help you, kid. You'll be sending me in there to fight a fire with nothing but air."

The lawyer was a Bronx native with a bad suit and a worse accent, but Marcus knew he was right. There was no reason on earth for a judge to take his word for it. On December 2, it was going to be either Charlie or him.

Who knew if the authorities would even believe the

truth? A fifty-four-year-old Alzheimer's patient didn't exactly fit the profile of a juvenile delinquent. They could accuse Marcus of trying to blame his own misdeeds on a sick, helpless man. That was easier to swallow than a wild tale of an NFL veteran mistaking a strange kid for his childhood friend and carrying on a grudge against a store that had gone out of business years ago. Unless by sheer luck the judge happened to be James McTavish himself.

The thought startled him. Okay, granted, the judge wasn't likely to be James McTavish. But James McTavish had to be somewhere. If Marcus could find the real Mac, then Mac could fill in the blanks.

Of course, the guy might live in California . . . or Japan. He might even be dead. But it wouldn't hurt to try to track him down.

There were two McTavishes in the Kennesaw white pages, neither of them James. One was an elderly woman who was hard of hearing. It was only with great difficulty that Marcus was able to gain her assurances that she had no relatives named James. The second guy was easier to communicate with but of no more help.

"Yeah, I remember hearing about other McTavishes somewhere in the area. They weren't part of our family, though. Sorry, pal."

Marcus did an internet search and found, to his dismay, that there were more than two thousand McTavishes in the United States. Nearly three hundred of these had the first initial J. And there was always the possibility that the J. McTavish he was actually looking for was unlisted.

The magnitude of the task at hand was beginning to sink in. Oh, sure, it could be done. But how did you go about it? What were the steps? Marcus was a high school kid, not a private detective.

He was about to shut down the browser when the message caught his eye:

WHO ARE *YOU* LOOKING FOR?

It was a banner ad for www.almamater.usa, one of those websites where people could track down former schoolmates, find old boyfriends and girlfriends, and reconnect with past acquaintances.

It brought an ironic smile to Marcus's lips. Himself and Troy, twenty years down the road, laughing over their long-forgotten animosities. Alyssa, now a farmer's wife, mother of six, former porn star, ambassador to Finland— anything was possible.

But it occurred to him that this was exactly the place he needed to be. He was looking for a high school classmate. Not his own, but Charlie's.

He entered the site and clicked on *Find an Old Friend*. He typed in the school's name and location—*David Nathan Aldrich* in *Kennesaw, New York*—and highlighted *Class of '73*.

In the space designated for his message, Marcus typed:

We played football together for the Raiders and in Three Alarm Park, when we weren't making trouble for Old Man Dingley. What happened to you, Mac?
                                                    —Charlie P.

As the mouse hovered over *Submit,* Marcus knew a moment of unease, pondering the possibility of the real Charlie P. visiting this site and finding a message from himself. But that wasn't very likely. If Charlie could look at a sixteen-year-old and see his friend Mac, then he wasn't searching for long-lost classmates. Part of him probably thought he was still in high school.

A grimmer thought occurred to Marcus. There was a decent chance that Charlie might be so impaired, he couldn't figure out how to use a computer at all.

CHAPTER
FOURTEEN

The Aldrich Raiders won again, despite an uneven performance from quarterback Troy Popovich. It was nothing that the average fan in the stands would recognize—he was just a touch quick to abandon the pocket. He got rid of the ball a little early, and he slid when he might have picked up a few extra yards by scrambling. But to Marcus, who had done all these things as a JV quarterback in Kansas to avoid getting hit, it was as obvious as blown coverage in the end zone. And there was no mistaking the worry lines on the bobblehead brow of Coach Barker—and around the luscious lips of the true football expert in Kennesaw, the head cheerleader.

It was hard to tell if Troy knew what was going on in his own head, or if the whole thing was subconscious. Marcus understood the cause of Charlie's problems, yet his association with the King of Pop had made him crave the very same kind of physical contact that Troy now seemed to be trying to avoid. Of course, Troy was Charlie's son, so the former linebacker's illness would affect him in a different and more profound way. He might even fear a genetic weakness that would make him prone to concussion.

In the end, though, Troy's mediocre game was more than made up for by the heroics of Ron Rorschach. Behind Marcus's ferocious blocking, Ron was en route to a rushing title, piling up touchdowns along the way. And he was already second only to Troy in the number of rhyming cheers designed by Alyssa and the squad.

Even Marcus was starting to get noticed, for the sheer energy of his physical play. The crunch of his hits could be felt in the back row of the bleachers. He was the secret of Ron's success, by far the best Raider rookie this year. But the nonfootball scuttlebutt was even more tantalizing: He had been arrested and given a court date to face criminal charges (true); he single-handedly fought his way out of Luke Derrigan's basement the night of the party (false); he rode a motorcycle (half true); he stole Troy Popovich's girlfriend and then dumped her (twenty-five percent true); the dumping part was just a cover, and he and Alyssa were still secretly seeing each other (totally false, but nice to think about).

Marcus tried to tell himself that he didn't care, but the fact was he did. He noticed the admiring looks in the hall and the whispered conversations in his wake.

Alyssa explained it with her usual flare. "Marcus, you are so hot right now, we could fry an egg on your pecs. And I found you first. Go, me!"

He would have taken her compliments more seriously if she didn't always make them among large groups of people, where they were pretty sure to work their way back to Troy. Yet the flirting felt great—and he couldn't escape the notion that, in spite of everything that had happened, it could get a whole lot better.

The problem was this: Alyssa the Football Expert understood blocking. He opened up holes so that Ron could gain yardage and become a star. In other words, Marcus did the donkey work in order for someone else to reap the rewards.

He had to wonder if he might be performing the same function outside football as well.

The email in the inbox of Charlie P.'s account on www. almamater.usa had the subject "Blast from the Past?" Hand trembling, Marcus clicked on the message and read:

> Is this really the Charlie P. I think it must be?
> My name is Doris Brennan Vanderboom, but

you probably remember me as Dori, who sat behind you in trig class senior year. I'm president of the DNA Alumni Association here in Syracuse, where many of us seem to have settled after college.

Because we're neighbors up here, our little group meets every few months for wine and cheese and to talk about the good old days. The purpose of this message is to see if we can cajole you into joining us sometime. We all followed your career in college and the NFL. What could be more delightful than having our football hero back in the bosom of his DNA fans?

I've checked the Association records, and the last address we have for you is in San Diego—decades out of date, I'm sure. Are you back in New York State? What do you say, Charlie? Are you too big a star to let a bunch of old friends fawn over you?

Hopefully yours,

Dori

Class of '73

Excitement dissolved into disappointment. Not Mac. Just some busybody from the alumni association. But really, what had he expected? To throw a posting on a message board and find the real Mac? It was too big a world for that. It was actually kind of amazing that he'd stirred up anyone at all from the class of 1973.

Not that Charlie cared. If the King of Pop gave a hoot about his old classmates, he'd have supplied an address more current than San Diego, which had to be more than twenty years old. . . .

Marcus put the brakes on his galloping mind. The California address was outdated, but it was still an address. Alumni associations kept information on everybody! His mind made the leap. If they had one for Charlie, then they probably had one for Mac, too. It might be just as old, but at least it was a place to start.

He turned back to the keyboard and typed a careful reply to Doris Brennan Vanderboom:

Dori,
    Good to hear from the old crowd. The Syracuse reunions sound great. Hope to get to one soon. I've been trying to track down my old friend James McTavish. Do you guys happen to have an address for him? Maybe Mac and I could come together.

With mixed feelings, he signed it *Charlie*.

Marcus had his answer within a couple of hours. Charlie was a real celebrity among his former classmates, so Dori was beside herself with joy at the possibility of hosting the King of Pop in Syracuse. He had the feeling that Dori nurtured a crush on Charlie that dated back long before he'd ever picked up an NFL football.

She provided hideously boring details about her three lovely children and her husband, a gastroenterologist and weekend fly fisherman. But Marcus only had eyes for the bottom paragraph:

> We haven't heard much from Mac. It's sad how people lose touch. The last address we have is 85 the Colonnade Way, Coltrane, NY.
>
> Good luck finding him. Hope to see you both soon.
>
> D.

Coltrane, New York. He knew from his rides with Mom that Coltrane wasn't that far—about halfway between Kennesaw and the foothills of the Gunks. It was maybe half an hour's drive, depending on how hard you pushed your Vespa.

CHAPTER FIFTEEN

Eighty-five the Colonnade Way in Coltrane wasn't a house at all. It was an old brick warehouse that had been converted to trendy shops, with offices on the second floor.

Marcus parked the bike and entered the building. Could this warehouse have been built on the site of Mac's house? He doubted it. The brick was ancient. But why would the alumni association have Mac living in Candle World or Hiker Heaven?

He checked the directory on a sign outside the door. It was under the professional listings:

206—McTavish, James, CPA

This wasn't Mac's home. It was his office.

He climbed the stairs, holding his breath in anticipation. This was Mac, the person Charlie thought Marcus was. It was hard to get his head around that.

As he stood in front of 206, working up his courage, he could not escape the feeling that this door was a time warp, with an older version of himself waiting on the other side.

He knocked on the door and entered. A young secretary looked up from her computer screen and smiled a welcome. "Can I help you?"

"Is Mr. McTavish in?"

"Yes, he is. Do you have an appointment?"

Marcus's face fell. "No. No appointment. But I really need to see him."

She frowned. "Well, could I tell him what this is about?"

"I need to talk to him about an old friend of his."

"What old friend?" came a voice from the back of the room.

Marcus turned. The door to the inner office was open, and there stood a stout balding man in his mid-fifties.

"Charlie Popovich," he said aloud.

The man looked surprised. "Now, there's someone I haven't seen in ages!" He sized Marcus up. "Are you Charlie's son?"

Marcus shook his head. "Just—a friend."

"Well, come on in," the man invited, "and let's talk about Charlie."

They seated themselves in the inner office.

"Mr. McTavish—"

"Mac," his host corrected him. "Everybody calls me Mac. Charlie started that, back when we ran together. What a couple of hell-raisers we used to be!"

Marcus couldn't hide an answering smile. "I'll bet Old Man Dingley thought so, too."

Mac let out a hoot of laughter. "In spades! He owned this hardware store, but he thought he owned the world. We passed by on the street—he called the cops. We made noise in the park across the way—he called the cops. It was like he had a direct line to the police station. But I guess Charlie already told you all that."

"Not exactly," Marcus tried to explain. "It's a little complicated."

Mac frowned. "Well, how could you know about all that if you didn't get it from Charlie?"

"You're right," Marcus confirmed. "It *is* from Charlie. But he's not telling me tales from the past. He's living it all now, still torturing Old Man Dingley."

"Dingley died years ago!" Mac exclaimed sharply. "What are you trying to pull?"

"There's a new guy—an exterminator—in the same store," Marcus explained. "Charlie thinks that guy is Dingley." He swallowed hard. "He thinks he's still sixteen years old. And—he thinks I'm you."

"Kid, you're not making any sense."

Marcus had known that he could never pull this

off without betraying Charlie's secret. And while he'd promised Chelsea he wouldn't spread it all over town— well, this was Coltrane, not Kennesaw. It was a hairsplitting distinction, but it didn't matter anyway. Marcus had to get himself out of trouble. He owed it to his future, but mostly he owed it to Mom. The impending court date was weighing heavily on her shoulders, just as the lawyer's fees were draining her savings. He'd overheard her on the phone, talking about inviting Comrade Stalin up north for a "loving intervention." Like the good comrade was any more capable of love than he was of interstellar travel. Still, the fact that Barbara Jordan would consider intentionally placing herself in the same room with the guy—the situation screamed for drastic action.

"The thing is, uh, Mac, there's no easy way to say this." He took a deep breath. "Charlie has Alzheimer's disease."

Mac was dismayed. "He's only my age!"

"It's the early-onset form of the disease, which is different," Marcus explained soberly. "They think it has something to do with football—too many concussions in a short period of time. It's happened to a few other NFL players."

Mac looked grave. "I read something about that, but I didn't think it was the same kind of Alzheimer's that old people get. I pictured these guys—I don't know— like Ozzy Osbourne minus the drugs. A little loopy from having their bells rung a few too many times." He smiled fondly. "Charlie could be pretty loopy all on his own, back in the day." The smile faded. "How bad is it?"

Marcus shrugged. "If you just hang out with him for a few minutes, you probably won't notice anything at all. But over time the weirdness comes out. Like, he considers himself my age, and he also knows he has a wife and kids. I'm not sure how much he understands and how much he's faking it. There are certain things that make sense to him—football, Three Alarm Park, you. Well, you meaning me. I think he might just bounce around until he sees something he recognizes. That's how we met. I was practicing in the park, and he just—joined in."

"Three Alarm Park," Mac said wanly. "The two of us practically lived there. How I survived those afternoons I'll never know. I used to watch Charlie in the NFL and think *I could be dead right now*. I knocked heads with that guy—with no pads!"

"How did you and Charlie lose touch?" Marcus asked. "You were so close in high school."

Mac shrugged. "Football—that's what brought us together. We both went to college at East Bonaventure— East Bumwipe, we called it. But you know how it is. Charlie had what it takes, and I didn't—not at the Division One level, anyway. I guess I resented it when he went on and I got cut. But some of it was just time. When you play college ball, that's your life. I wasn't in the locker room, or on the bus rides, or in those cheap hotels. We weren't on the same planet anymore."

He shook his head. "When he got drafted by the Chargers, I thought I'd give anything for that to be me. But what you're telling me—wow."

The phone rang, and Mac called to his secretary to take a message.

He faced Marcus once again. "No disrespect to Charlie, kid, but why come to me with this? Yeah, I'm the real Mac, but apparently not in Charlie's eyes. I'm sorry an old friend's got trouble, but there's not a heck of a lot I can do about it. He needs a doctor, not a CPA."

"I've got a problem," Marcus admitted, a little ashamed of pushing his own self-interest. "Charlie has it out for this guy he thinks is Dingley. It's just pranks, but you know Charlie. He's relentless. And the cops have decided that I'm the one who's doing it. Now I've got a court date and vandalism charges on my record, and I can't defend myself without siccing the cops on a poor guy with Alzheimer's."

"Well, there you go," Mac told him readily. "Charlie's got a perfect excuse. He's not liable because of his condition."

"Great," Marcus said bitterly. "So I'm not just ratting him out for who TP'ed the store. I'm telling the whole world that he's losing his mind."

Mac shook his head. "You can't take all that on your shoulders. It isn't fair. You've done nothing to this exterminator fellow, and you shouldn't be blamed for it. You don't even know that you're doing Charlie a favor.

You help keep his illness a secret, and maybe the next time he visits Dingley's old store, he falls down the stairs and breaks his neck. Is that going to be your fault, too?"

Marcus nodded sadly. "I don't even know if anyone'll believe me. It's a lot to swallow—that Charlie is living in the past, and he thinks I'm you."

Mac's face lit with understanding. "So that's why you're here. You need me to back you up about Charlie's old life. Why didn't you say so?"

"I'm not proud of it," Marcus mumbled. "I've only known him a few weeks, but when we were together, I *was* Mac. He *made* me you, complete with all the years you guys were friends. That must sound strange—"

The CPA shook his head. "Makes perfect sense. That's Charlie. He pulls you in. The power of his will shapes everything and everybody around him. Even more than his football skill, that's what got him to the pros. Nice to hear he's still got it. Especially considering the circumstances."

Marcus studied his sneakers. "I feel like I'm stabbing him in the back."

Mac handed over his business card. "If you have any problems, send the cops to me. I'll do whatever I can to set the record straight."

"Thanks," said Marcus gratefully. "Just from the way Charlie talks to me as Mac, I knew you'd be a good guy." He pocketed the card and stood.

Mac walked him to the door. "Funny you should show

up now of all times. I've been thinking about Charlie lately. I just got the notice about the hall of fame thing."

Marcus goggled. "Charlie's going to the Hall of Fame?"

Mac laughed. "Not the NFL one. The one at our old college. Hey, don't knock it. They had a real good football program back then. Every year they induct a few people to their sports hall of fame, and this time Charlie's on the list."

"Awesome!" Marcus exclaimed. "Charlie'll love that."

Mac looked dubious. "Are you sure he'll understand what's going on?"

"You know, I really am. The two things that make the most sense to him are football and the past. Anyway, even if he doesn't get all the details, you can't misunderstand a crowd of people cheering for you."

Mac nodded. "Well, I'll be there. I haven't gone to homecoming in decades, but this one I won't miss."

CHAPTER SIXTEEN

The stands rocked with the roar of fans who smelled blood. The Raiders clung to a seven-point lead, and the Rhinebeck home crowd howled for their Giants to put an end to Kennesaw's unprecedented winning streak.

As the offense clattered off the field, the players were greeted by an enraged Coach Barker. "Who called that time-out? I'll kill him! In case you haven't noticed, this is a close game!"

Troy flopped onto the bench. "*I* called it. Didn't you see that hit? Helmet to helmet! Where's the personal foul?"

Barker handed him a water bottle. "Incidental contact, Popovich. No harm done."

"Maybe not to you!" The quarterback's voice was rising. "He nearly took my head off! I've got ringing in my ears!"

"We've all got ringing," the coach soothed him. "If these people would shut up, it would go away—and we'd have half a chance to hear our own signals!"

"I was right there," Marcus told Troy. "He barely touched you."

"If you're such a great blocker, how come he touched me at all?" Troy rasped. "Something's definitely wrong. I think my vision's blurred."

Barker called for Dr. Prossky, who served as team physician. He was actually an oral surgeon, but he was such a huge Raiders fan that he traveled with the team to all the away games. As the doctor examined Troy, shining a penlight into his eyes, Marcus watched the time-out clock. Their thirty seconds ticked down.

He pulled his helmet on. "I'll finish the series—"

"Not so fast." Barker cast him a look that would have melted steel. "Applegate—take over at QB."

"But *I'm* the backup!" Marcus blurted.

"I need you to block! Now get in there before we lose yards for delay of game!"

You had to pity the poor linebacker who tried to get at Calvin on the next play. Marcus hit him so hard that his helmet rolled to the far sidelines. By that time, Troy had been pronounced healthy, and even he was willing to admit it.

"I don't have to explain my decision to anyone," Barker told Marcus later on the sidelines. "But you're a good kid, and I owe you this much: If I put Calvin in, what I've got is a couple of wasted downs. I put you in, and I've got a quarterback controversy. Take pity on me, Jordan. Too much talent isn't always a good thing."

In the end, the Raiders managed to hang on, although the seven-point margin of victory was the slimmest since the beginning of perfection.

As the team celebrated, Coach Barker was not smiling. Neither was Marcus.

Still, a win was a win, so their history-making hopes continued to be on track. The team hadn't lost since 2007, when Poughkeepsie West, the other local power, had beaten them in overtime. The next meeting with West, two weeks away, was considered the biggest threat to the Raiders' quest for a place in the record books.

Barker's strategy was out in the open now. Harmony over everything, keep the peace at all costs. The coach had to see that Troy's game was falling apart, but he was convinced that pretending nothing had gone wrong was preferable to replacing the guy with somebody better. Last year's squad had been world-beaters; a similar roster would yield similar results.

By Barker's unspoken decree, Marcus no longer practiced at quarterback. He was helping the team—his blocking was legendary, his cornerback coverage rock solid. But he took no snaps at the afternoon workouts.

Calvin ran the backup QB's drills, and even those were kept to a minimum. Nothing could be allowed to eat away at Troy's fragile confidence.

In contrast, Marcus's other roles were actually expanding. Barker had already recruited his blocking prowess for the kick-return unit. On Wednesday, the coach began to experiment with blitzing Marcus from his cornerback position. He was a natural. On the very first scrimmage, he steamrolled over Ron like his backfield mate was a speed bump, and charged in on the quarterback.

Somewhere in the corner of his mind was the vague feeling that this was going to be a satisfying, revenge-drenched sack. But that was secondary to his football player's intense singleness of purpose—to make the play.

His eyes locked on Troy. The guy was a sitting duck—no scrambling, no evasive action, a deer in headlights. He was just standing there, waiting to get creamed. And the look on his face—pure terror.

Coach Barker blew the whistle so hard that hands flew to ears to muffle the painful sound. The effort of pulling up practically imposed g-force on Marcus. But he couldn't hit the guy. He just couldn't.

After practice, in the locker room, Marcus was stepping out of the shower, a towel wrapped around his midsection, when he found himself bare toe to bare toe with Troy, similarly attired.

Coming upon one's adversary armed only with a few square feet of terry cloth had a *High Noon* feel to it. Their dislike for each other was magnified by the fact that there was nothing but white tile and porcelain to distract them.

For Marcus, the moment was doubly uncomfortable. Any Popovich was a reminder that he still hadn't amassed the courage to tell Officer Deluca about Charlie. He knew he had to, though, especially now that he had Mac to back him up. It was inevitable—the sooner the better, before Charlie did something else and left Marcus to take the rap again.

Yet standing there in the locker room, Marcus was amazed to feel genuine sympathy. The sack-that-never-was had taken the edge off Troy. It was tough to hate the titan you'd just seen cowering like a helpless child. Minus godhood, Troy wasn't the enemy. He was just an ordinary jerk—one who deserved a little slack because something pretty damn awful was happening to his father.

With effort, Marcus found something civil to say. "I heard about your dad's honor. Great news."

Troy's eyes narrowed. "What are you talking about?"

"The hall of fame."

The quarterback shook his head. "You're some sick bastard to make fun of my father. Considering what you know—which is *none of your business*—"

"The one at his old college," Marcus interrupted, flustered. "East Bonaventure."

"What have I ever done to you?" Troy demanded icily. "My father, my girlfriend, my team. Even my sister— you're like her new hero for dragging him home from the park! Why don't you get your own life and stay out of mine?"

Marcus was shocked speechless as Troy stalked away. It wasn't the hostility that surprised him. It was the fact that Troy seemed so totally blindsided by his father's upcoming honor. How could he not know? Was it possible that Troy was so affected by his father's illness that the family wouldn't even discuss Charlie with his own son? How would they explain it to Troy when they took Charlie to EBU homecoming for the induction ceremony?

Then another thought occurred to him. An awful thought.

Marcus found Chelsea at her locker before school the next day.

She was now the friendlier of the Popovich children, which was to say that she no longer reacted like a pit viper every time she saw him. Still, she was wary as he approached, greeting him with a quiet "Hey."

"Hi, Chelsea. Listen, I have a question for you, but you've got to promise not to bite my head off."

She regarded him dubiously. "Okay."

He took a deep breath. "Does your dad read his own mail?"

She bristled. "You know, Troy says you have an unnatural obsession with our family, and maybe he's not wrong."

Marcus stood his ground. "I wouldn't ask if it wasn't important."

"He passed second grade a long time ago. Yes, he knows how to read. If you have a point, please make it, because you're starting to get on my nerves."

"Charlie is being inducted into East Bonaventure's sports hall of fame in two weeks."

She was impatient. "No, he isn't! Don't you think his own family would know if—" She stopped short when the significance of his original question dawned on her. Was it possible that Charlie had received the letter and forgotten about it? Or hadn't understood it in the first place?

Her face seemed to crumple, and he spoke up quickly. "Hey, this is *good* news! You should be happy your dad's getting the recognition he deserves."

It did nothing to reassure her. Marcus could read the fear in her eyes. These days the family's central preoccupation was keeping on top of Charlie's unpredictable behavior. Just when they thought they were in control, here was something important that they had no idea about. It had to be pretty scary.

Aloud, she said, "How come we're always learning about Dad from you?"

Marcus shrugged evasively. "I heard it from another

EBU alum. This guy's all excited to see your dad get honored." He could almost taste her mistrust. "I promise I'm not stalking you guys. I just wanted to make sure you knew about it. It's a great thing for Charlie."

Elizabeth Popovich sat at the computer, her son and daughter peering over her shoulders at the East Bonaventure University website.

"It's true! They're inducting your father and the Rogers sisters into the hall of fame!"

Troy scowled. "Who are the Rogers sisters?"

"A synchronized swim team," Chelsea supplied. "It says they won the Olympic silver medal back in 'eighty-eight."

"Dad's in real good company," her brother sneered.

"Never mind that!" Mrs. Popovich snapped. "How could we not know about this?"

Chelsea couldn't restrain herself. "I hope you're kidding, Mom! I can't believe that after all we've been through with Daddy, you don't know the answer to that question!"

"I've been to all the doctors' appointments!" her mother exclaimed. "I've read enough about Alzheimer's disease to earn a PhD. But my husband of more than twenty years would *not* forget something like this."

"He didn't forget," Troy said bitterly. "To forget something, first you have to have a clue about it."

Chelsea looked daggers at her brother. "This is our

father you're talking about."

"No, it isn't," he muttered. "It hasn't been him for a long time."

"Could it be the school's fault?" Mrs. Popovich mused. "They could have misplaced the letter. Or the post office . . ."

"Dream on, Mom," said Troy. "Who knows what he's doing with his mail. Probably eating it."

"He reads!" Mrs. Popovich shot back hotly.

Chelsea shook her head. "He does things out of habit. Maybe he's just looking at pages."

Her mother stood up. "We need to find that letter. Where does Dad keep his mail?"

The five-bedroom house had a spare room that Charlie used as a study. There were a desk, a leather chair, and bookshelves, all in pristine condition.

"See?" Mrs. Popovich's enthusiasm was forced. "Look how tidy he is. Is this the office of a person with a disorganized mind?"

Chelsea patted the chair cushion, and a small puff of dust rose. "No, it's the office of someone who doesn't come anywhere near his office."

There was no mail of any kind on the desktop. A search of the drawer revealed eight broken pencils and a desiccated sandwich with a slice of what had been turkey covered in greenish fuzz.

Mrs. Popovich was horrified. "I think that's from last Thanksgiving!"

"That's from the *first* Thanksgiving," Troy amended sourly.

Chelsea tried to stay focused. "Okay, so he doesn't come here. Where *does* he go?"

"Do I look like his travel agent?" mumbled Troy.

"You know what I mean. He sits on the porch. He putters around the garage. If we can figure out the place, we can search for the mail."

"It has to be the porch," Mrs. Popovich decided. "I sort through the mail, hand him his, and he goes out front to read it."

Troy got a strange look on his face. "The glider track on the porch swing has been sticking since the summer. . . ."

The three rushed out the door and approached the swing like it was booby-trapped. Chelsea got down on her knees, pressed the seat back, and reached into the housing of the glider track. When she withdrew her hand, she was clutching a fistful of mangled envelopes.

"It feels like there's a ton of it back there," she reported.

Mrs. Popovich began to sob.

"Ease up, Mom," Troy said gruffly. "This is nothing new."

"It's just . . . so hard . . . to know for sure when the little slips and forgetful episodes really add up to something more serious."

"You know when the doctors tell you," Chelsea replied

gently. "When there are so many slips that they all blend together—"

"And when your porch swing is full of mail," Troy added.

Mrs. Popovich nodded, ashamed. She had once been queen of real estate in this town. Now she needed her son and daughter just to force her to see reality.

Chelsea was trying to smooth out crumpled dirty papers. "Oh—this one's from last April," she groaned. "How are we going to reach the stuff that's crushed at the bottom?"

Troy headed for the garage. "I'll get a tire iron. Maybe we'll find my letter from Santa in there."

Soon they had the glider track pried open. An amazing sight met their eyes. The box was crammed full of mail in various stages of shredding and decomposition. Some pieces were little more than pulp, mashed by the moisture in the air and the to-and-fro of the mechanism.

They began to sort through the envelopes, working in silence. The image of what had happened was clear to all of them—Charlie opening his mail, skimming the contents, then getting distracted and stuffing the letters under his seat to look at later. But later never came, and instead the mail was ground into the track by the motion of the swing.

At length, they found the envelope that bore the EBU logo, postmarked June 29.

Dear Mr. Popovich,

Congratulations! We are pleased to inform you that you have been selected for induction into East Bonaventure University's Sports Hall of Fame.

Your achievements in the National Football League have been an enormous source of pride to everyone in the East Bonaventure community, and we are delighted to bestow upon you this well-deserved honor.

We hope that you will be able to join us for the ceremony, which will be held homecoming weekend, November 14 . . .

"He knew about it," Mrs. Popovich breathed.

"He knows nothing," Troy said firmly.

"But the letter was opened."

"Even if he read it twenty times, he knows nothing about it now."

"Troy's right, Mom," Chelsea agreed in a small voice. "What are we going to do?"

Troy shrugged. "We'll go through all this mail to make sure he didn't throw out anything else important. We'll try to fix the swing—" He stopped and stared at his sister. "You mean the *ceremony*? What good would it do to take him there?"

"It's Dad's honor," Mrs. Popovich reminded her son. "He's earned it."

Troy was appalled. "You want to honor Dad? Let him keep his dignity instead of parading him in front of all those people so they can see exactly what he's turned into!"

Chelsea was angry. "You don't care about his dignity! You just don't want him to embarrass the Great Troy Popovich!"

"If he goes to this thing," Troy said tersely, "do you honestly think he'll understand word one of what's happening to him? Of course not! All we'd be doing is sticking him in a car for two hours, confusing the hell out of him, and sticking him back in the car for the return drive."

"Is that what you really think?" Chelsea challenged. "Or is it just because the date clashes with the Poughkeepsie West game?"

"If you don't trust what I think, why don't you ask your *boyfriend*?" Troy challenged. "Since he knows Dad so much better than any of us do!"

"Well, Marcus thinks he *should* go. So maybe he *does* know Daddy better."

Mrs. Popovich seemed torn. "I look in his eyes and I still see the man I married. Maybe I just want it too much . . ."

Troy put an arm around his mother's shoulders. "You think I wouldn't give anything to have the old Dad back?"

"They'll send a plaque, right?" she mused sadly. "He'll

like that. That'll be a pretty big honor."

Chelsea nodded, eyes moist. "Yeah."

There were footsteps on the front walk, and Charlie leaped athletically onto the porch. "Hi, guys. Hey—who broke the whatchamacallit?"

CHAPTER SEVENTEEN

East Bonaventure University is pleased to welcome synchronized swimmers Stephanie and Elise Rogers back to their alma mater for this year's induction ceremony. . . .

Marcus stared at the words on the EBU website. Stephanie and Elise Rogers? What about Charlie? Surely the King of Pop rated at least equal billing with a couple of nose-plug jockeys from 1988.

Of course, Charlie's response would have gone in late—good thing Marcus had gone to see Mac in Coltrane or the Popovich family never would have found out about the ceremony in the first place. The next time EBU updated its website, surely they'd be welcoming Charlie, too.

He sat back in the hard wooden library chair and peered through the window at the passing parade in the school hall. Quite a few eyes turned toward him, and there were plenty of smiles and waves. There was no question that he'd made an impact as a football player, even on the you-can't-improve-perfection Raiders. It still bugged him that he would never get a chance at quarterback when he was the best choice for the job. But there was plenty to be proud of besides throwing touchdown passes.

I love the pop!

He spied Alyssa among those who waved, but in her case, the gesture was accompanied by a lot of body English. If it was possible to hit on someone in half a second from the other side of reinforced safety glass, she aced it. A moment later, Chelsea entered his field of vision, in the company of a few sophomore girls. He tapped on the window to get her attention. She looked toward the source of the sound, nodded a very cursory greeting, and turned away quickly. He tapped again. This time she picked up her pace and hurried past.

Okay, he wasn't exactly at the top of the Popovich family Christmas card list. But there was something more. As he slid his chair back along the carpet, the web page headline swept into view . . . and he just knew.

Charlie's omission from the homecoming roster had nothing to do with a late acceptance. He hadn't been mentioned because he wasn't going.

Marcus raced out of the library just in time to see Chelsea disappear into the cafeteria.

He caught up with her in the food line and wasted no words. "You're not taking him."

"Not here," she mumbled under her breath.

"I can't think of a better place," Marcus returned quietly but firmly. "Somewhere too public for the lecture about how this is none of my business."

"It *is* none of your business," she hissed.

Maybe, but he wasn't about to let it go—not with something this important on the line. "Explain it to me anyway."

She abandoned her tray at the taco bar and headed to a deserted table.

Here it comes, he thought. *She's really going to let me have it.*

Instead, she just said, "I'm sorry, Marcus."

"I'm not the one you have to apologize to," he told her. "That would be your dad."

She reddened. "If we take him there, he won't understand. It'll just get him mixed up to the point where he could freak out in front of everybody. "

"You don't read minds," Marcus argued. "No one can be one hundred percent certain what's going on in Charlie's head."

"It's not up to me," she said defensively. "It's up to my mom."

"Are you sure it isn't up to Troy?"

"That's out of line!" she snapped. "I know you have a problem with my brother. I have a problem with him, too. But we're my dad's family, and you're not. A couple of months ago, you'd never even met Charlie Popovich. How dare you act like you know *one fiftieth* of what it's like to watch your father turn into a lost, helpless stranger?"

Marcus had no reply. She was one hundred percent right.

"It's a family decision," Chelsea went on. "Mom thinks Daddy would just get upset. And you know what? I agree with her. Why drag him across the state for nothing?"

"Sorry to bug you," Marcus mumbled stiffly. He left her to return to the taco bar and exited the cafeteria.

Okay, so Marcus had no business meddling in their family's crisis. And yet—

He knew Charlie in a way that neither his wife nor his children did. As Mac, he'd seen Charlie from a friend's perspective. Sure, the relationship was based on a fundamental misunderstanding. But that didn't mean it wasn't real. Too real—Marcus was facing criminal charges because he didn't want to rat Charlie out.

Over the past month, a lot of Charlie-and-Mac had seeped into Charlie-and-Marcus. Charlie and Mac had been kids together, football buddies, hell-raisers, closer than brothers. Now Charlie was about to miss out on the biggest honor of his life.

What would Mac do?

Chelsea said Charlie wouldn't understand the hall of fame induction. Maybe, maybe not. Marcus could sit in the cafeteria all day and debate the issue with her.

Or he could confront the one person who could provide the answer for real.

It felt strange to be in Three Alarm Park in the middle of the school day. Not that he had a huge guilt complex about ditching class. But he couldn't get past the thought that if Officer Deluca found him here now, he'd be arrested for truancy instead of the usual vandalism and harassment. That would certainly pad his bad-boy legend at school.

The park wasn't as empty as it had been during the summer. There were a few young mothers pushing babies in strollers, and an elderly couple chatting on a bench in the shadow of the Paper Airplane. *Remembrance*—what a name for the sculpture that marked his first meeting with a guy who couldn't remember at all.

No, that wasn't quite right. Charlie *did* remember. He remembered what still made the most sense to him—being young and wild and invincible, taking on the world with his best friend. Those memories were so pure and vivid that he believed he was still living them in the here and now.

Marcus had already made a few circuits on the Vespa, but there was no sign of his onetime football pal. Of course, it was a long shot to expect to find someone by running into him on the street. Still, he knew that Charlie, in his confusion, often spent his days prowling this area in search of something familiar.

Come on, Charlie, where are you?

Eventually, he knew, he'd have to go back to school. But before that, he decided to make one final run along Poplar Street toward Seneca Hill, where Charlie lived.

He hadn't left the park far behind when a commotion reached his ears. Angry voices filled the air around a bus parked at the curb on the corner. A small lineup of passengers shuffled impatiently as the driver ordered a tall, belligerent man off the bus.

A familiar voice announced, "I paid my quarter, and I'm entitled to my ride!"

"That's not a quarter, it's a walnut! And the fare's two bucks, mister!"

"Two bucks? What is this, a bus or a stretch limo?"

"It's neither!" roared the driver. "It's the shuttle to the outlet mall."

Marcus leaned the Vespa against the fence and ran up. "Hey, what's going on?"

Charlie regarded him in irritation. "Back of the line, pal!"

The driver shot Marcus a desperate look. "You know this guy, kid? Is he your dad or something?"

"Or something," Marcus acknowledged non-committally.

"You've got to get him some help," the driver pleaded. "This isn't the first time he's done this. At least I'm used to him. If it happens on my day off, he could wind up at the outlet mall with no idea how to get home again."

"Come on, Charlie," Marcus said gently. "Let's go."

"You don't tell me what to do!" Charlie protested. "I don't even know you!"

"Sure you do—I'm Mac."

"Mac?" He looked a little less angry, a little less sure of himself.

Marcus reached further into his storehouse of topics that might trigger recognition. "Just be careful. Old Man Dingley's on the warpath." He took a chance and grasped Charlie's arm.

Charlie allowed himself to be led down off the bus and along the sidewalk toward Three Alarm Park. As the scenery grew more familiar, he became animated.

"I say we take every nail in the store and dump it in the middle of the floor! Let him spend the rest of his life sorting."

"Later," Marcus promised. "Listen, I've got to ask you something."

Charlie hopped up on a concrete bench and began to walk effortlessly along the narrow back. "Fire away."

"Do you know what EBU is?"

"Sure." The reply was instantaneous. "East Bumwipe, where I played my college ball."

"Good times?" Marcus probed.

"The best. You were there."

"That's right," said Marcus, choosing his words with

the utmost care. "We're the same age, right?"

"Three weeks apart," Charlie confirmed, wobbling slightly before regaining his balance.

He thinks he's my age, yet he knows he had a college career. He sees no logical flaw in remembering university in the past while being in high school in the present.

Things didn't have to make sense to make sense to Charlie.

Marcus took a deep breath. "One last thing. How would you feel about EBU inducting you into their sports hall of fame? Would you go back for the ceremony?"

The former linebacker jumped to the ground. "Are you kidding? What ballplayer wouldn't?"

Marcus turned it over and over in his mind, but the facts always lined up the same way:

Charlie *had* to be there for his hall of fame induction.

His family wasn't going to take him.

I have to get him there myself.

It was no minor thing. For starters, Marcus would have to miss the Poughkeepsie West game, which everybody said was the most important matchup of the year. Worse, he couldn't even warn the team he'd be a no-show, for fear of inviting nosy questions. He'd worked so hard to carve out a spot for himself on the Raiders squad. He'd be putting all that in jeopardy.

As tough as that was going to be, it was small potatoes compared to the difficulty of disappearing for a whole day with a guy who had Alzheimer's. Definitely not the kind of stunt you could pull off without anybody noticing. The hall of fame ceremony was scheduled for halftime of the EBU homecoming football game. Even if they left right afterward, at the start of the third quarter, it would still be an absence of five hours, minimum. Charlie's family allowed him some freedom, but they'd begin to worry when he was gone for so long—just as they had worried the night of Luke's party. And when they realized where he was—and who he was with—well, then it was really going to hit the fan.

Like I'm not in enough trouble already!

Marcus couldn't even feign cluelessness. Chelsea had already told him the family's decision and the exact reasoning behind it. Payback was going to be a monster, especially if Mrs. Popovich called the police. Marcus's relationship with local law enforcement wasn't exactly the best. He could only hope that Charlie himself would back him up.

If Charlie even remembers the ceremony by the time we get home . . .

He shook his head to clear it. It was reckless and stupid—and totally the right thing to do. It made no sense for Marcus. Yet *Marcus as Mac* had to deliver his "old friend" to EBU, and damn the consequences.

Deliver was the operative word here. East Bonaventure was 110 miles away. Marcus couldn't ask a man with Alzheimer's to hang off the back of a Vespa all that way.

They needed another form of transportation. To borrow the car from Mom, he'd have to explain where he was going. And coming up with the right lie was beyond him at the moment. Besides, he couldn't risk her getting in trouble for this by providing the vehicle. That kind of mess would be Comrade Stalin's dream. He could have her declared an unfit parent—he'd threatened to do so often enough. Then the good comrade could sue for— *God forbid!*—custody.

But how else could he get Charlie to homecoming?

"Marcus!" exclaimed the hearty voice of James McTavish over the phone. "Good to hear from you! Did you get that little legal problem ironed out?"

"I'm working on it," Marcus replied. "Listen, uh, Mac. You said you were thinking about going to EBU for homecoming and the ceremony. Is that still the plan?"

"Wouldn't miss it. Been thinking about the old days ever since you came to visit."

Marcus cleared his throat carefully. "Any chance of Charlie and me catching a lift with you?"

Mac sounded surprised. "Charlie doesn't drive?"

"Not anymore," Marcus replied. "Too much chance he might get lost, I guess. He could wind up three hundred miles from where he should be."

"But surely his family wants to see him inducted?" Mac persisted. "His wife?"

"His son has a big football game that day," Marcus

explained, grateful for a little truth upon which to build his dishonesty. "They're working on a second perfect season. Kennesaw is obsessed with it."

"I've heard about the Raiders. I should have guessed Charlie's son might be on that team. Never could light a fire under my own boys to take much interest in football. They see me creaking around on two bad knees. . . ."

"So can you drive us?" Marcus asked anxiously.

"Sure," Mac agreed. "It'll be great to see Charlie again—even if he thinks you're me and I'm some old cue ball from the Stone Age. Where do I pick you up?"

Nervously, Marcus gave his own home address. He couldn't risk Charlie's family seeing him leave in a strange car. And a neutral location like Three Alarm Park might seem suspicious to Mac.

Now all he had to do was make sure the most unpredictable guy in town presented himself at exactly the right place at exactly the right time.

CHAPTER EIGHTEEN

The screen door clattered open and Troy appeared on his front porch, shrugging into a Raiders letter jacket. "Hurry up, Chelsea!" he shouted over his shoulder as he walked out to his car in the driveway.

"Give me five minutes," his sister called from a second-story window.

"I'm not waiting!" Troy got into his Mustang, started it with a roar, and began to honk vigorously.

A few seconds later Chelsea rushed out, simultaneously brushing her hair and trying to stuff her backpack. The argument between Troy and his sister happened every morning, as dependable as the sunrise. This was a mild

170

one. Usually Troy was halfway down the block, racing the engine and shouting through the sunroof, while Chelsea ran along the sidewalk, begging him to wait.

From his hiding place four houses down, Marcus could not make out her angry words to her brother as she jumped in the car and they squealed away. It was the third straight day that Marcus had staked out the Popovich home. In order to make sure that he'd be able to find Charlie on November 14, it was important to chronicle the man's routine—if there even was one. Alzheimer's patients were, by definition, erratic. And yet even animals, without the benefit of wristwatches, fell into patterns of behavior that put them in the same place at the same time, day after day, doing the same thing.

Sure enough, there was Charlie, right on schedule, coming out to sit on the porch swing. As always, he had the paper under his arm, but his attention to it consisted of a brief glance at the front page. Then he set it on the cushion beside him and began methodically peeling a banana. This was new. The last two days, breakfast had been a bagel. As he began to eat, he absently tucked the peel underneath his seat, where it was immediately ground into the glider track. Yuck.

Marcus squinted. Why was Charlie wearing a puffy bomber jacket? It was a warm fall day, probably headed to the low sixties, and he was dressed for the North Pole. The thought had barely crossed Marcus's mind when Mrs. Popovich appeared. She exchanged her husband's winter gear for a light windbreaker, kissed him on the cheek, and went back into the house. A few minutes later, Charlie stood, performed a few warm-up stretches, and left the porch at a jog.

Marcus started the Vespa and followed along at a discreet distance. So far, so good. Charlie always went the same way—downhill, in the direction of Three Alarm Park. It was in town that the route would begin to vary. Different distractions would pop up, and it was impossible to predict which of these would attract his attention and take him off course. It could be as simple as music coming from an open car window or a line of people at a bus stop or the hot dog cart. The man was naturally drawn to lineups. Marcus thought this might be a rare glimpse into his disease. A group with a clear purpose had to be attractive to someone who could never quite recall the nature of his own. It was kind of sad.

On the other hand, Charlie didn't seem unhappy. He didn't even seem lost. Every now and then, he'd be ecstatically greeted by someone who recognized the town celebrity. That had to increase his sense of belonging. He took it all in stride and was charming and friendly to everybody—even the ladies who tried to flirt with him. Marcus would have given a lot to know what was going on in Charlie's head at those moments. If he thought he was a teenager, what could his opinion be of these middle-aged bats who were old enough to be his mother?

He checked his watch nervously. Five minutes to first

period. He had already missed history two days in a row. No way could he cut again. If the office called his house to see what had happened to him, Mom would hit the roof. He had already put her through so much with the impending court case, and the worst was yet to come. The fallout from November 14 was likely to be enormous—and he knew she would try to take the brunt of it for him. That was just the way she was.

A plan formed in his mind: Go to school for history class, then cut second period and come back to see if he could reacquire Charlie. It was a good test—to see how hard it would be to find his quarry on the move, rather than always starting out from Charlie's home first thing in the morning.

An hour later, he was on the bike again, not coasting but pushing the motor flat out, speeding toward town. He tried Three Alarm Park first, and then began to cruise up and down the nearby streets. No Charlie.

He began to sweat. How could he even consider a plan like homecoming if he wasn't truly confident he could produce the man of the hour?

He continued the sweep, working his way outward from Poplar Street until stores and businesses were less common. The small downtown ended, and the neighborhood became increasingly residential.

A muffled banging reached his ears over the Vespa's engine. At the bank branch on the corner, a tall man stood pounding his fist against the ATM.

Marcus rode up and jumped off the Vespa. "Charlie— what's wrong?"

The King of Pop turned around in outrage. "I didn't get my gum!"

"Your *gum*?" Marcus examined the machine. An error message flashed on the screen. An unhealthy buzzing sound was coming from the card slot, where a small coin had been jammed inside.

"I paid my dime, and I want my gum!" Charlie stormed.

"It's not a candy machine," Marcus tried to explain.

Charlie delivered another wallop to the cash door. "Well, what's it for, then?"

Gently, Marcus placed a hand on Charlie's arm and led the former linebacker half a step away from the bank.

"I know you from somewhere," the King of Pop said uncertainly.

"I'm Marcus. Marcus Jordan."

Charlie's eyes found the Vespa. "That your bike? I've been thinking of getting one. My car . . . I don't know where my car is."

"Want a ride?" Marcus swung a leg over the scooter and slid forward in the saddle to make room for Charlie to join him. Then he gunned the throttle. The supercharged bike rocketed past the buildings and storefronts of downtown Kennesaw. Charlie let out a whoop of exhilaration, feeling the wind whipping through his curly hair.

Marcus felt like whooping himself. He had finally figured out how he was going to get Charlie over to his house for the ride to EBU.

As they skirted the fence surrounding Three Alarm Park, Charlie peered over Marcus's shoulder and took in the familiar trees.

"Hey, Mac," he shouted over the roar of the engine, "how come you never told me you've got a motorcycle?"

CHAPTER NINETEEN

November 14 was sunny and breezy, perfect weather for the Poughkeepsie West game—and East Bonaventure's homecoming.

Marcus sat astride the Vespa at the end of Charlie's street on Seneca Hill, tearing his hair and fuming. Where was Charlie?

He checked his watch, not for the first time. Ten after nine. In the entire two weeks that Marcus had been staking Charlie out, never once had the man left his house any later than eight thirty. What a day for an unexpected change in the routine!

In twenty minutes, Mac was going to pull up to the

Jordan home to drive Marcus and his old friend Charlie to EBU. And nobody would be there.

What was going on? Were the Popoviches keeping a tighter rein on Charlie now? Understandable, but why start *today*? Every other morning Charlie went off on his own and, by design or by accident, he always found his way home. From the perspective of the family, today was no different.

Something must have happened.

But what?

The noise coming out of the speakers was painful and earsplitting—a cross between audio feedback and an animal roar.

It brought Chelsea running down to the basement. "Daddy, what are you doing?"

"The stereo's broken!" Charlie shouted over the din.

She stared. "No it isn't!"

There on the old-fashioned turntable sat a gleaming silver CD, being scratched and mangled by the diamond stylus on the tone arm. She lifted the needle off the disc, and blessed quiet descended on the house. "This isn't a CD player. It's for your old vinyl records."

"I knew that," said Charlie stoutly.

"Here—this is from your collection." She selected a Rolling Stones album from the rack, slid the record from its sleeve, and set it on the turntable.

As the familiar guitar chords began to play, her father

perked up. "Now, *this* is rock and roll. Thanks."

Chelsea tossed the ruined CD into a wastebasket. "Enjoy." She headed back upstairs.

Her father settled in to listen to the music. When the record ended, he became aware of another sound—a persistent tapping. Bewildered, he turned around until a face at one of the windows high on the basement wall caught his eye. A teenager was beckoning frantically.

Charlie pushed open the slider. "What do you want?"

"Come on!" Marcus stage-whispered. "We're late!"

"Well, let's go." He didn't have a clue what they might be late for, but there was no mistaking the urgency in the newcomer's voice. This had to be important.

He took the basement stairs two at a time and strode to the door, a man of purpose.

Mrs. Popovich looked up from her laptop computer. "Oh, I thought you were already out for your run."

"I'm late," Charlie explained briskly.

"Well, don't stay out too long. Don't forget we've got Troy's football game this afternoon."

"Got it," Charlie promised, shrugging into his EBU warm-up jacket. The face at the basement window was already gone from his mind as he hit the porch running and started off down the street. He didn't even notice the teenager waiting for him half a block away. He only looked up when he heard the Vespa's engine rev.

The smile on Marcus's face was one hundred fifty percent relief. "Hi, Charlie. Hop on."

Charlie hesitated. "Do I know you? I don't know you."

Marcus kept his voice steady. "Sure, you do. I'm taking you to the homecoming game."

Charlie brightened. *Right. The football game.*

He climbed onto the back of the Vespa. "Is this just a little putt-putt, or has it got some guts?"

Marcus twisted the throttle, and they were off. He drove fast, but not out of any need to impress Charlie. Mac believed he was picking up Charlie at the Popovich residence. The last thing Marcus needed was to invite questions about where they were coming from.

When they got to the Jordan house, Marcus barely had time to stash the Vespa in the garage before a silver Toyota Avalon tooled up to the curb. Mac jumped out, beaming. In a voice that was at the same time excited and reticent, he exclaimed, "Charlie, I'd have known you anywhere!"

Watching them, Marcus was trembling in his boots. What in the world was Charlie going to think of James McTavish? He certainly wasn't going to recognize this bald, middle-aged accountant as his friend Mac.

But Charlie breezily replied, "Yeah, good to see you," and got right into the passenger seat of the car. If he was confused, it didn't show.

Mac looked at Marcus over the top of the Avalon. "How's he doing today?"

"So far, so good," Marcus replied. "He knows he's

going to homecoming. But it can't hurt to remind him a lot."

Mac nodded. "We'd better get moving. We're bringing the guest of honor, and he shouldn't be late." He folded his long legs under the wheel. Marcus climbed in the back, and the Toyota pulled away.

Marcus had wondered about the conversation during the two-hour drive. What could these two possibly find to talk about?

He needn't have worried. Mac had brought along an old cassette tape of East Bonaventure University's fight songs.

Marcus watched, transfixed. As soon as the music came on, Charlie's lips began to move. After a few bars, he was singing word-perfect with the lyrics.

Amazing! The guy's memory was in tatters, yet he had perfect recall of school songs he hadn't heard in more than thirty years.

Mac joined in, and soon the Avalon reverberated with the sound of two old guys bellowing off-key, but more in tune with each other than the voices of the Mormon Tabernacle Choir.

The song dissolved into a chorus of belly laughs. Mac wiped his eyes, one hand on the wheel. "You know where I found this tape? It was propping up the short leg of my workbench in the garage! This is priceless stuff! It brings back college like it was yesterday!"

Marcus kept an eye on Charlie. Because of his

Alzheimer's, the King of Pop might think all that really *was* yesterday. "Popovich and McTavish," he put in carefully. "A devastating combination."

"Sure were!" Charlie exclaimed. "Just ask Old Man Dingley. Remember the time we dumped out every nail in the store? He's probably still sorting!"

Mac chuckled appreciatively. "Remember when he chased us with his riding mower and knocked over that policeman's wife in the phone booth?"

"That was a classic!" Charlie howled. "He almost went to jail for that! And he'd just barely forgiven us for the time we put a football through the window of his car!"

Mac chuckled. "Funny—I don't remember that one."

"*I* do," said Marcus pointedly.

"Oh—oh, yeah," Mac acknowledged.

The conversation rollicked on. Wild football parties in both high school and college; cheerleaders with great legs; beer-chugging linemen who could belch the Pledge of Allegiance without taking a breath. The real Mac was at the wheel, and the teenager Charlie took to be Mac was over his shoulder in the backseat. Somehow Charlie was able to combine the two and satisfy himself that he was in the company of James McTavish. All this reminiscing was completely genuine.

"Forget all that," Mac roared. "Yours is the stunt that will go down in history. The Harrison game? The hawk?"

The look that appeared on Charlie's face was like

nothing Marcus had ever seen there before. It wasn't just that Charlie remembered—he remembered a lot of things, especially from the distant past. It was the sheer, unholy glee of this recollection—it transformed him from a middle-aged man into the crazy kid he sometimes believed he still was.

Marcus sat forward eagerly, leaning into the split between the front seats. "What happened?"

"You had to be there," Mac supplied. "You had to know about the rivalry between our school and Harrison. They had this mascot—a hawk they called Harry. Just listening to it scream was worth your eardrums. God, we hated that bird. We hated that whole team. But it took Charlie to work up the diabolical plan to do something about it."

"It was no big deal," Charlie put in. "I just stole the cage, that's all."

"You're leaving out the best part!" Mac insisted. He continued the narrative. "There's a big dispute on the field, so nobody sees him. Next thing they know, Charlie's charging up the bleachers with the cage under his arm. All of a sudden, the whole Hawks team is going after him. Everybody's screaming, especially Harry. Those guys were going to kill you, right in front of our home crowd!"

"I just had a job to do, and I did it," Charlie said modestly.

"Which was . . . ?" Marcus prompted, wrapped up in the story.

"Picture this," Mac said with relish. "This crazy

lunatic is at the very top of the stadium, tightrope-walking on the wall behind the last row of bleachers. I swear—a single gust of wind and he's a grease spot on the hood of somebody's car in the parking lot! It's so damn scary that even the Harrison guys stop chasing him."

Marcus could relate. He pictured Charlie perched precariously atop the Paper Airplane, and on various fences and ledges around Three Alarm Park. Even now, the guy had a natural tendency to pick the highest, most precipitous spot in town and go dancing.

Mac continued to set the scene. "Total silence in the stadium. And what does this maniac do? He starts singing 'Born Free' and pops the cage. The bird takes off into the wild blue yonder and is never heard from again."

"Did you get in trouble?" Marcus asked breathlessly.

"Only for the rest of my life," Charlie replied. "That's how long it took to pay for the new hawk. Who knew those things were even for sale?"

"Did you at least win the game?" Marcus asked.

"Nah, we got killed," Mac admitted with a grin. "Nobody beat Harrison. But I'll tell you—from then on, I never once set foot on that field—even for graduation— without looking up to the back of the bleachers, half expecting to see Harry finally making his way home." He turned to his high school friend. "It must have been like that for you too, huh, Charlie."

"Yeah . . . right," murmured Charlie, suddenly vague. "Who's Harry?"

Mac was shocked. "The bird—Harrison's mascot!"

"Right . . . the mascot . . ."

Marcus checked his watch. "Do you think we have time to stop for a snack or something? I think a soda or a coffee would do us all some good."

Charlie rebounded after pie and coffee at a truck stop about forty miles from their destination. He and Mac even reminisced about the greasy spoons and roadside luncheonettes the EBU Bears had frequented on their road trips. This included a diner outside Syracuse where the entire team had picked up food poisoning from the turkey chili, ". . . and let me tell you, the quarterback got more than he bargained for from the center."

Thirty years of no contact—plus Charlie's illness—could not interfere with the capacity these two men had to laugh together.

Mac glanced at the clock on the wall. "I don't want to break up a good party, but we've got another party to go to. Let's hit the head and then hit the road."

A few minutes later, Marcus stepped out of the men's room and left the restaurant to join Mac, who was already standing by the car.

"I see what you're talking about," Mac confided soberly. "One minute it's the old Charlie who hasn't changed since high school. But then it's like somebody flips a switch. You look in his eyes and there's nobody home."

184

Marcus nodded. "I know. I really appreciate your doing this, Mac."

"Don't thank me. I should have done it years ago. I don't see where he thinks you're me, though."

"That seems to happen more around Three Alarm Park," Marcus mused, "where everything is familiar. But in the car, he's got your songs and stories."

Mac nodded. "I wonder what he's thinking now—strange bathroom, no familiar faces."

Marcus suddenly looked stricken. "He's been in there a long time. . . ."

The two ran back into the restaurant and flung wide the bathroom door.

"Charlie!" Marcus called with rising dread.

The stalls were all empty, the fluorescent-lit room deserted. A wide-open window told the tale. For reasons known only to himself, and probably already forgotten, Charlie had run away.

CHAPTER
TWENTY

Mac was bug-eyed. "He *escaped*? From *us*? Why?"

"Not from us!" Marcus was breathing so hard, he was gasping out the words. "At the moment he took off, he probably didn't even remember we were here! Let's just get him back, okay?"

They ran outside again, looking around desperately. There was no sign of him.

Mac was completely bewildered. "Do you think he went into the woods?"

"I hope not!" An athlete like Charlie, with a head start in forested terrain, would be very hard to find.

But Marcus doubted that the King of Pop was headed

for the deep woods. He generally gravitated toward what was most familiar. A highway would make more sense to him than wilderness.

Mac pointed down the road. "Oh boy—"

A quarter mile away in the direction they'd come from, a tall figure strode along the soft shoulder, thumb up. Charlie was hitchhiking.

With one mind, Marcus and Mac started running toward him, screaming at the top of their lungs.

"Charlie! . . . Wait! . . . Over here! . . . Charlie! . . ."

It was no use. Their voices were not reaching him. They watched in agony as a long-distance eighteen-wheeler came rumbling along the highway. At the sight of the hitchhiker, the driver began to gear down.

Mac was horrified. "Don't do it, pal!" he breathed.

Marcus could not wrap his mind around the potential disaster that was unfolding before him. If this truck picked Charlie up, he could be three counties away within the hour.

The indecision almost shattered him. Should they run faster? Head back for the car and a chance at pursuit? Memorize the truck's plate number to supply to the police?

He watched helplessly as the driver got a good look at Charlie and decided against picking up this stranger who looked every inch the linebacker that he was. With a roar of its big diesel engine, the big rig sped on by.

"I'll get the car!" Mac wheezed, reversing field

toward the rest stop. "Don't take your eyes off him for a second!"

Moments later, the Toyota pulled alongside Marcus, and he jumped into the backseat.

Mac was worried as they sped to where Charlie was walking backward, still hitchhiking. "What if he doesn't recognize us?"

"It won't matter," Marcus reasoned. "He's hitching. We're giving him a ride. Just pretend we're total strangers."

Mac closed the quarter-mile gap and rolled down the passenger window. "Where are you headed?"

Charlie was momentarily unprepared for that question. "Home," he said finally. "In the United States."

"That's exactly where we're going," Marcus assured him. "Hop in."

It was as simple as that. Charlie sat down in the passenger seat, and they were off again.

Mac lobbed an uneasy glance over his shoulder at Marcus. "Maybe we should be heading toward—uh—the United States right now. You know, home."

Marcus had been expecting this. It was one thing to accept that Charlie had Alzheimer's, but this was Mac's first life lesson on how a little confusion could quickly spiral into a dangerous situation.

"It's just a couple of hours," he pleaded. "This might be the last chance he ever gets to be—his old self. We'll be more careful. We can handle it."

"Doesn't his wife know how serious it is?" Mac murmured. "If I was her, I wouldn't let him out the front door."

"I don't think he's so bad around his family. You know—same house, same people. There's a lot about it on the internet. Unfamiliar surroundings make the confusion worse. He probably looked around that bathroom, saw nothing he recognized, and lost it."

"You may be right," Mac conceded. "But every mile we drive gets us that much farther from the familiar. What then?"

"Put the tape on," Marcus urged. "The EBU fight songs."

Charlie, who had been gazing out the window oblivious to their discussion of him, suddenly came to life. "EBU? I went to EBU."

"Me, too," mumbled Mac, now subdued. "Small world."

He popped in the tape, and the music did the rest. Soon Charlie was singing, which lightened his friend's mood.

"You know, it's homecoming today," Marcus ventured from behind him.

"No kidding." Charlie looked wistful. "I wish we could go."

"It's your lucky day," Mac said ruefully, pushing a little harder on the accelerator.

■ ■ ■

Troy Popovich jammed the last of his gear into his gym bag and swung the huge duffel over his shoulder.

His mother watched with a jaundiced eye. "Why do I bother? I'm so careful to iron your clothes and to fold them, and for what? So you can wad them up like used Kleenex."

Troy shrugged. "So don't bother." He looked around. "Where's Dad?"

It drew Chelsea from the next room. "He's not back yet?"

"I'm sure he'll be here soon," her mother assured her. "He knows about Troy's game today."

Brother and sister exchanged a look of silent exasperation.

"Ever wonder which of our parents is the one with the brain damage?" Troy whispered.

"Not funny!" Chelsea admonished.

Mrs. Popovich sighed. "Well, he knew this morning, and I think he deserves the benefit of the doubt. Has he ever missed one of your games before?"

He made a face. "You don't seriously believe he's got a clue who he's watching, do you?"

"The two of us talk about how you're doing through-out the whole thing."

"Okay," Troy said, "but what if he didn't have a living, breathing cheat sheet sitting right next to him? Would he know then?"

"Get out of here before I hit you," she told him, not

unkindly. "Go to your team lunch."

"Do you remember what time it was when Daddy went out this morning?" asked Chelsea.

"A little after nine."

Chelsea checked her watch. Ten fifty-five A.M.

CHAPTER
TWENTY-ONE

Whatever was or wasn't going on in Charlie's brain, when he arrived at EBU, it was obvious he was experiencing a homecoming unrelated to the event that was being celebrated that day.

He leaned forward in his seat, looking around, taking in the ivy-covered buildings with their weathered stone facades.

He remembers, Marcus thought excitedly. *He knows this place.*

"Well, here we are," Mac announced as they moved along the tree-lined drive. "Looks a lot smaller than I pictured it all these years. What do you think, Charlie?"

Charlie peered straight ahead, frowning in concentration. "There's a fountain—right there."

They followed his pointing finger. There were young people standing around a building that appeared to be a dorm or student center. No fountain.

Marcus and Mac exchanged a knowing glance.

"We should find the stadium," Mac decided. "It's almost—"

"A fountain," Charlie insisted. "With a guy on a horse in the middle of it."

All Marcus's anxiety returned. Was Charlie *hallucinating* now?

The Toyota passed the dorm, continued beyond a clump of white birch, and there it was.

Mac nearly cheered. "A fountain! And a statue of a guy on a horse!"

"Hey," said Charlie, "I used to whiz in that fountain. You don't forget a thing like that."

"Jeez, I think I might have been with you!" Mac exclaimed.

They ran into a traffic jam as they approached the stadium parking. But then Marcus spied a sign: VIP LOT.

"That's right," Mac chortled triumphantly. "We don't have to wait with the common people. We've brought the King of Pop!"

There was a little confusion at the gate because they weren't on the list, until Mac announced, "Don't you know who this is?"

The attendant regarded Charlie quizzically for a moment, trying to place the vaguely familiar face. And then a middle-aged woman with a HOMECOMING COMMITTEE CHAIR badge came bounding over.

"Charlie Popovich! Why didn't you tell us you were coming! Everybody's going to go *crazy!*"

The attendant was impressed. "Yeah? You're Popovich? I used to watch you play! Can I shake your hand?"

Within a few minutes, Charlie was mobbed by well-wishers.

Marcus watched like a proud parent. The fact that he had made this possible absolutely thrilled him. It was easily the most worthwhile thing he had ever done.

He was so wrapped up in the moment that it took a few seconds to realize that the committee was walking away with Charlie.

Mac was already on it. "Number one rule," he told the committee chair. "We go where he goes."

"I'm afraid that's not possible," she explained reasonably. "There's a limited amount of space on the dais—"

"No deal," Mac replied firmly. "You're not hearing me. We can't leave him alone."

She tried to make a joke out of it. "Are you his bodyguards?"

"Something like that."

Eventually, Marcus and Mac were seated two rows behind the honorees—close enough to lay hands on Charlie if they felt they must.

Charlie was between the Rogers sisters and EBU's president. As word spread that the NFL veteran had turned up unexpectedly at homecoming, a procession of fans and old classmates paraded by.

Marcus marveled at the way Charlie greeted each one with a firm handshake and a hearty "Good to see you!" No one ever would have suspected that *this* Charlie was anything less than what he appeared to be—a celebrity, the center of attention, the man of the hour.

Mac nudged Marcus. "Look at him. An hour ago, he climbed out of the toilet and tried to hitchhike to the United States. Now he looks like he's running for governor."

Marcus nodded. "He's really pulling it off."

But could it last?

Chelsea ran into the house, slamming the screen door behind her.

"Is he here?"

Her mother appeared in the kitchen doorway. "You didn't find him."

"I went all over town, all his usual haunts. Even Three Alarm Park."

Her mother checked her watch. "It's only lunchtime. Troy's game isn't until three."

"This isn't about the game!" Chelsea exploded. "Daddy's like a bear who wanders into the middle of New York City! He could get hurt; he could hurt someone else—"

"I'm worried, too," said Elizabeth Popovich sharply, "but he's been gone this long before. He's always come back."

"Except the time Marcus had to go rescue him," Chelsea reminded her.

"That was *one night*. There's no reason to believe it wasn't an anomaly."

"We hid his car keys when the time came," Chelsea argued. "What if we've passed the point where he can't be left on his own at all? And now it's too late?"

"Don't panic, Chelsea. Your father isn't a bear in New York; he's a man in the town he grew up in."

"Well, what about Troy? Shouldn't we let him know Daddy's still missing?"

Her mother thought it over. "Not yet. We don't know for sure that anything's wrong. We don't want to get him upset right before the biggest game of the year."

Chelsea stomped into her room, fuming. She understood that her mother was trying to think positively, but a couple of drops of water didn't mean the glass was half full! How could she be so *calm*? The night of Luke's party, if it hadn't been for Marcus, who knows *what* might have happened?

Marcus. That was the person to call. Of course, her father wasn't at Three Alarm Park now. But maybe Marcus would have another inspired guess based on the special relationship he seemed to have with her dad.

There was no answer at the Jordan house, so she tried

Marcus's mother at the newspaper office.

"Mrs. Jordan, my name is Chelsea Popovich. I'm a—a friend of Marcus's. Sorry to bother you, but it's kind of important. Do you have any idea where I can find him?"

"I don't think I can help you," Mrs. Jordan replied. "He told me he was going to be away all day at a football game."

"Poughkeepsie West," Chelsea supplied. "I'll probably see him there. Thanks anyway."

She hung up, frowning. The game didn't start until three. It would be over by five, five thirty at the latest. There was nothing "all day" about that. Why would Marcus tell his mom—?

No. Impossible. It couldn't be.

DNA versus Poughkeepsie West wasn't the only football game going on that Saturday. It was also homecoming at East Bonaventure University. That was a pretty long drive, so he would've had to leave early, and by the time he got back . . .

She ran to the computer and called up the university's website. Right there on the home page was a live-streaming video feed from the homecoming game—EBU versus Rutgers.

She checked the notice board about the hall of fame inductions to see if any "special guests" had been added. No, it was still just the Rogers sisters. Charlie Popovich was listed as an absent honoree.

I must be losing it, she told herself. *How paranoid do*

you have to be to think some kid shanghaied your two-hundred-forty-pound father?

She focused on the live stream—players from both teams were diving after a fumble. EBU recovered, and the crowd went wild. The camera panned the spectators, focusing on faculty and guests in a bunting-draped box.

The shriek brought her mother running from downstairs.

"What is it, Chelsea? Are you all right?"

"I found Daddy," she replied shakily.

"What are you talking about? Where?"

"There!" her daughter quavered. "Look!"

The two watched the computer screen in amazement as Charlie jumped up and down, cheering and waving an EBU pennant.

Mrs. Popovich goggled. "How did he get to East Bonaventure?"

Chelsea was furious. "I told him he had to respect our decision!"

Her mother was bewildered. "Who?"

The camera pulled back and supplied the answer. Charlie sat down again, providing an unobstructed view of a spectator seated two rows behind him.

Marcus Jordan.

Officer Deluca hung up the phone and let out a long, sharp breath. In twenty years of police work, he thought he'd heard it all, but this was something new: a sixteen-year-old kid abducting a fifty-four-year-old Alzheimer's patient to take him to the hall of fame ceremony his own family wanted him to skip. For reasons of their own, he assumed.

Had he overlooked anything? Oh, yeah—also, the suspect was Marcus Jordan, who had been in town only a few months yet was not unknown to the Kennesaw Police Department, and who was ticking down to his own court date for vandalism and harassment.

He sighed. To go from TP'ing an exterminator's shop to kidnapping an NFL veteran was quite an escalation, even for the Jordan kid. Of course, he wasn't holding the man for ransom. He just took him to a football game. Still, in the eyes of the law, it was a full-fledged abduction, especially in light of Popovich's condition. Another shock, that. The pride of Kennesaw had Alzheimer's at only fifty-four. Poor guy.

He looked through his Rolodex and dialed the number of the Bonaventure County Sheriff's Office. Luckily, Sergeant Earl Ewchuk was on the desk—an old friend of Deluca's from the academy days.

"I need a favor," Deluca told him. "Charlie Popovich— remember him? Played for the Bengals. He's up your way at the EBU game right now."

"Yeah, I heard he's here," Ewchuck told him. "It's quite a surprise at the college. They weren't expecting him."

"That's probably because he's not supposed to be there."

"What are you talking about, Mike?" Ewchuck demanded. "They're honoring him at halftime—him and the nose-plug sisters."

"I know he's invited, Earl, but he's a sick man. Too many concussions, the wife told me. And the person who brought him snuck him out of town against the family's wishes."

"You got an ID on this guy?"

"Never mind him," said Deluca. "He's a sixteen-year-old kid. And besides, he's in the stands two rows behind Popovich. That's who I'm worried about."

"I'll call the campus cops and have him pulled out of there," Ewchuk offered.

"Don't. Let him have his moment in the spotlight. But keep an eye on him. He can't leave. I'll be there in a couple of hours."

"Done," Ewchuck promised. "See you then."

Deluca hung up the phone and reached for his car keys. On top of everything else, he was going to miss the Raiders game against Poughkeepsie West. Two perfect seasons on the line, and he was going to spend the afternoon chasing an Alzheimer's patient and Marcus Jordan over hell's half acre.

The kid had a lot to answer for.

CHAPTER
TWENTY-TWO

Both Rogers sisters had put on a few pounds since their silver-medal days—the same amount, of course, almost to the ounce. But their bright smiles and synchronized waves were just the same as they stood on the rollout stage at midfield, accepting the accolade of their alma mater.

Then the scoreboard screen faded out from the 1988 Olympics medal ceremony and into the image of a young linebacker in EBU crimson. The number on his jersey was 55. Long hair poured out of his helmet, but his wild, intense stare burned through the cascading curls like halogen headlights cutting fog. His posture radiated energy and strength, and when he moved, it was with explosive quickness and athletic grace.

A buzz rippled through the crowd as the voice-over traced the career of Charlie Popovich—first his four stellar years at EBU, and then later as a pro in San Diego and Cincinnati.

From his seat in the grandstand, Marcus watched Charlie, who was standing quietly at the edge of the stage, eyes riveted to the scoreboard monitor. Did he know he was watching himself? Or was he just interested in a story about a football player? It was impossible to tell.

"Students and faculty, please welcome our other hall of fame honoree, the King of Pop himself: our very own Charlie Popovich!"

The roar that greeted this announcement moved air. The crowd rose to its feet, stamping and cheering East Bonaventure's NFL star. The grandstand glittered with thousands of camera flashes. It was pandemonium.

With some prodding from EBU's president, Charlie stepped to center stage, and Marcus felt his stomach tighten into a nervous pretzel. Beside him, Mac sat forward, his body stiff and tight. What would Charlie say? How would he react to finding himself the focal point of tens of thousands of people? Marcus and Mac waited, scarcely breathing.

"It's great to be back at good old East Bumwipe!"

That drew an outburst of laughter and a standing ovation that took several minutes to quiet down.

"The last time I stood on this field, I had a broken

nose, and Mary Frances Gilhooley's underwear was flying from the flagpole," Charlie went on. "I know because I put it there—me and a friend. What I'm trying to say is, the days I spent right here were some of the best times of my life. And to come back and be honored for it—well, that's just gravy."

"Look at his face!" Marcus breathed. "He gets it! He gets *everything*!"

Mac was pink with emotion. "To think I almost turned back!"

"Thanks, everybody," Charlie concluded. "I'll never forget this."

The cheers were deafening.

Two large tears rolled down the cheeks of Elizabeth Popovich. "You see that?" she said to her daughter. "*That's* your father."

Chelsea nodded. "I barely remember him this way."

Her mother wiped her eyes. "I don't think I realized how far gone he is—not until now, seeing him the way he used to be."

"He looks happy." Chelsea turned suddenly angry. "How come that jerk Marcus always knows more about Daddy than we do?"

"I've been so blind!" Mrs. Popovich exclaimed. "You and Troy told me again and again, but I wouldn't listen!"

"Don't think about that now," Chelsea sniffled. "Look—it's a standing ovation."

■■■

As the cheering roared on, Marcus and Mac got to their feet, leaping and high-fiving in triumph, their words an incoherent babble.

For Marcus, the exhilaration was double. The plotting, the machinations, the split-second timing—it was all worth it for this incredible moment. His life had become a muddy chaos of negative emotions: bitterness toward Stalin, regret for Alyssa, anger at Troy, resentment for Chelsea and Coach Barker—and even Mom, for moving him out of Kansas. Yet this felt astonishingly different— simple, crystal clear, and one thousand percent *right*.

On the field, the grounds crew was rolling the stage back to the sidelines. The ceremony was over, and the second half would soon begin. The Rogers sisters, flushed with pleasure, were being escorted back to their seats and—

Marcus froze. "Where's Charlie?"

It took all the wind out of Mac's celebration. "Don't tell me we lost him!"

Marcus mentally plotted a course from the 1988 medalists back to midfield. No Charlie anywhere along that route.

"What was he wearing?" Mac prodded urgently.

"An EBU warm-up jacket!"

They both looked around in dismay. Three quarters of the crowd was clad in East Bonaventure crimson— jackets, sweatshirts, even stadium blankets.

They ran, sprinting down the concrete steps to ground level.

"Hey!" bawled a security guard. "You're not allowed on the field!"

"Where's Charlie Popovich?" Mac demanded.

"Back to your seats!"

Marcus spied Charlie on the opposite sidelines, walking into the tunnel at the center of a cluster of people.

"There!" he shouted, and vaulted over the half wall onto the turf. Mac was barely a step behind him. They raced across the gridiron, dodging the entire Rutgers Scarlet Knights offense, jogging out for the third quarter.

"Charlie, *wait!*" bellowed Marcus.

By the time they reached the mouth of the tunnel, Charlie and the group surrounding him had disappeared.

They pounded down the passage, shouting Charlie's name. Marcus spun a three-sixty. The hall that led to the locker rooms was deserted. Another led to equipment storage. The third choice was a door that opened onto the VIP parking lot.

Marcus crashed through the heavy door. The King of Pop wasn't in the lot. Frantically, he expanded his search field. It was a busy homecoming Saturday at EBU. People were everywhere in the distance, strolling on walkways and relaxing on benches and blankets.

Mac burst onto the scene, shouting, *"Charlie—"* He scanned the bustling campus. "Uh-oh."

Marcus was in an all-out panic. "We could pick a direction and look there, but it would be pure luck if we found him!"

"All right, stay calm," counseled the CPA. "Let's try to think like Charlie."

"You *can't* think like Charlie!" Marcus raved. "His mind is totally random!"

"Not necessarily," Mac argued. "When it's sunny, he shades his eyes, right? His impulses are the same as anybody's. If he's hungry, he'll look for a hot dog stand. If he has to pee, he'll look for a bathroom. . . ."

There was a momentary silence as they recalled the conversation on the drive across the campus. Then the two Macs looked at each other.

"The *fountain!*"

They took off in a full sprint, with Marcus in the lead. It was at least half a mile. Marcus made it in record time, and even Mac was puffing along, not far back. There was the fountain, but no Charlie. Marcus was distraught. They had gambled and lost. In the time it had taken to run here, and the time it would take to get back to the stadium, Charlie could be anywhere on the vast campus—or worse still, off campus. What if he hitchhiked again—or boarded a bus bound for Syracuse or New York City?

Unaccustomed to the half-mile race, Mac struggled to regain his breath. Heaving, he turned to a student who was sitting on the rim of the fountain, reading. "Have you seen a guy—a big guy, about my age—tall—curly hair—"

"Wait—he was with you?" the young woman exclaimed.

"He was here?" Marcus blurted.

"He sure was," she replied. "He stood there for a long time, staring up at the statue. Then he stepped over the edge and started walking toward it—right through the water! When he got there, he was climbing up on the horse—"

"Where is he *now*?" Marcus interrupted.

She grinned nervously. "He got arrested. It took, like, six campus cops to drag him down."

"Oh my God," moaned Mac.

"No, this is good," Marcus insisted. "It means he's okay." He turned back to the girl. "Where would they take him?"

She pointed across the quad. "The redbrick building. Campus security."

And they were off and running again. Now Marcus's fear for Charlie's safety was replaced by a less urgent but definitely more ominous feeling. Any chance of getting the King of Pop to and from EBU under the radar was gone with the wind. Marcus had always known he'd have some explaining to do. But he hadn't anticipated it would begin so soon.

This time, the older man's stamina was near its end, and Marcus opened up a quarter-mile lead, galloping for the security station. He blasted through the doors to find Charlie himself sitting on a bench, wrapped from the waist down in a heavy blanket.

"Marcus Jordan"—a voice that was definitely not Charlie's.

Marcus wheeled to find himself face-to-face with Officer Mike Deluca. He returned his attention to the King of Pop. "You okay, Charlie?"

The former linebacker looked from one face to another, sensing conflict and not much liking it. One thing was certain: The *old* Charlie, the real one, was no longer present. It was more than likely, Marcus reflected sadly, that he had already forgotten the honor of just twenty minutes before, the one he'd said he would never forget.

"He's fine," said Deluca. "He's with me. *I'm* the good guy. I don't know what to call you anymore. Kidnapper, maybe?"

Mac reeled onto the scene in time for this last part. "Nobody's been kidnapped!" he wheezed. "Charlie needed a lift, so we drove him."

Deluca glared at him. "And you are . . . ?"

"James McTavish."

Charlie stared at his high school friend. "You're not Mac! You're old!"

Mac indicated Charlie's reflection in the front window. "We're the same age, Charlie. Three weeks apart."

Charlie rounded on Marcus, frowning. "But you're—"

Marcus shook his head, devastated. "My name is Marcus Jordan." How could this day have gone so wrong? He and Mac had just taken the fundamental misunderstanding at the core of all Charlie's confusion and rubbed it in the poor guy's face. "I'm sorry."

He turned to the policeman. "Mac had nothing to do with this. He doesn't even know Charlie isn't supposed to be here."

Mac's eyes widened in shock. "What are you saying?"

"What he's saying, Mr. McTavish, is that Charlie's family knew nothing of his whereabouts until they saw him streaming live on the EBU website. That's when they called me to report that he'd been abducted."

Marcus gulped. "It's my fault."

Mac couldn't believe it. "You mean Charlie's family wanted him to *miss* this?"

"They were pretty specific about it to Mr. Jordan," Deluca replied, stone-faced. "Then again, Marcus never has been one for doing what he's told."

"Maybe he did something wrong, but he did it for all the right reasons," Mac argued. "You can't arrest him for being loyal to his friend—our friend."

The officer looked exasperated. "Do you see anyone being arrested here? Mr. Popovich is safe and sound and on the way home to his family. But just think about this—what if something had happened to him beyond wet feet? Whose fault would that have been? His own? I don't think so."

Marcus and Mac exchanged an agonized glance. The

nightmare scenarios were all too easy to imagine: Charlie falling from the statue, knocking himself unconscious, and drowning. Or wandering off, soaking wet, as hypothermia set in.

"The family has the right to file a complaint," Deluca went on. "I'd be well within my job description to cuff the both of you and stick you in the back of my car. So if you're not under arrest, it's for no other reason than you were damn lucky—"

"I've got to get home," Charlie interrupted, his voice plaintive. It was obvious that he was very tired. "My mom's going to be mad."

Mac stared at his old friend in sadness and sympathy.

"Tell you what," Deluca said to Charlie gently. "These fine folks have some dry clothes for you to change into. Then you can get in the back of the squad car, where you can stretch out and relax. I'll have you home in no time."

And you can't escape from a police cruiser, Marcus reflected grimly.

"We'll follow you," Mac decided. "Come on, Marcus. Homecoming's done."

Marcus nodded. Truer words had never been spoken.

CHAPTER TWENTY-THREE

The bleachers at Aldrich High School's football field were a fraction the size of East Bonaventure's stadium. But the stands were jam-packed, and the excitement became even more supercharged as kickoff time approached.

The town of Kennesaw had bought into the story of their Raiders one hundred percent. But Poughkeepsie West had sent four busloads of their own supporters, so they were well represented. There was an epic feeling about this game—the DNA juggernaut against the team that had last defeated them. The single major obstacle in the Raiders' quest for double perfection. An old rivalry ratcheted up to fever pitch.

Chelsea looked around the facility as if it had been designed to house some incomprehensible alien custom on a distant planet. Although she went to school just a few hundred yards away, she hadn't set foot in this place for more than a year. Ever since it had become apparent that football was the cause of her father's problems. The fact that Troy still played the sport—and their parents came to watch—made about as much sense to her as the medieval custom of tipping your own executioner.

She found her brother on the sidelines, scanning the general area of the stands where the Popoviches normally sat. The last time she'd watched him play, his pregame concentration had been so absolute that he'd barely even noticed there was a stadium around him. The contrast was striking.

"Troy."

He spun around, startled to see her. "Where is he?"

She almost smiled. Her brother was alternately angry, impatient, and sarcastic about their father's condition; he was constantly bugging Mom to stop bringing him to games. But deep down, Troy was twice as heartbroken as anybody. Sometimes that was the only thing that kept her from hating him.

"He's going to be late," she said evasively.

"What do you mean 'late'? What's going on?"

"Walk with me. The whole world doesn't need to hear this." They moved a few feet away toward the visitors' bench. "Listen—don't freak out. Daddy went to homecoming at EBU."

"Don't give me that! How would he even get there?" His eyes widened. "Your boyfriend?"

Chelsea reddened. "He's not my boyfriend. He's a dead man when I get my hands on him."

"Jordan blew off our game, stiffed the team, and took Dad a hundred miles on that scooter thingie?"

"I think he dug up some old friend of Dad's and they went together. Anyway, Daddy's fine. The police have him, and they're driving him home."

"Why the cops? Now everyone's going to *know*!"

"How could we not call them?" Chelsea demanded. "You turn on the computer and see your missing person streaming live from across the state! What would *you* do? If he wandered away from there, he'd be gone forever!"

"What the *hell* was Jordan thinking?"

She shrugged helplessly. "He thinks he knows what's best for our father. And I'll tell you something. Today he was right."

"What are you talking about?"

"The hall of fame," she insisted. "Daddy totally got it. Wait till you see the video clip!"

"Big deal, he got it!" Troy snorted. "Tell me he gets it *now*. Tell me he even remembers it."

She was adamant. "I guarantee he doesn't remember it. That's not the point. Our father achieved a lot in his life; he had the right to be honored for it. That's what Marcus Jordan understood and we didn't."

"He's got you, too! The guy is like a cancer! He tries out for the team, and pretty soon everything revolves around him, including Alyssa! He randomly meets our father, and now he's the real family, and we're out! What next? Is he going to move in with us? How long before we have to go?"

Chelsea regarded him in alarm. Did her brother notice that his voice was rising and even shaking a little?

Ron came up behind him and slapped him on the shoulder pads. "Hey, Coach wants us to—"

In one startled motion, Troy wheeled and threw a punch that resounded off the halfback's Plexiglas visor with a sharp *thwack*. A helmetless Ron would have been out cold.

"My hand!" cried Troy, grasping his fist in pain.

"What's with you, man?" Ron was furious. "Coach just sent me to tell you we're starting!"

"I broke my hand!"

That brought Barker running, with Dr. Prossky hot on his heels. The team gathered around as the oral surgeon performed his examination.

"No harm done," the doctor pronounced. "No swelling, just a little redness."

"What happened?" the coach demanded.

"Nothing," said Ron swiftly. "It was an accident."

"No accidents on game day!" Barker roared.

Troy tried to grip a football. It dropped from his nerveless fingers. "I can't!"

Dr. Prossky was dubious. "I don't see anything wrong."

"What if a knuckle's broken?" Troy persisted.

"Unlikely. Not without swelling."

Coach Barker took his quarterback aside. "Popovich, is there something you want to tell me?"

"I can't play," Troy replied, shaken.

"Dr. Prossky says you're fine."

The quarterback did not meet his eyes. "I can't play," he repeated quietly.

No official decision was made to follow Officer Deluca and Charlie all the way back to Kennesaw. Yet there was Mac, Marcus at his side, right on the squad car's tail.

"I think Charlie might be asleep," Mac commented. "He's dropped out of sight, so he must be lying down."

Marcus was buried in guilt. "I'm sorry about this, Mac. I was just so focused on getting Charlie to EBU that I never thought I might get you in trouble with the cops."

"Don't take this the wrong way," said Mac, "but if you don't stop apologizing, I'm going to have to throw you out of the car. Honest—I wouldn't have missed this for anything."

"It was stupid," Marcus muttered. "I mean, the risk! We could have ended up in jail."

"You know, Marcus, some things are worth the risk. I don't know if I would have said that yesterday, but I believe it now. It's more than just the hall of fame. That was the old Charlie back there—the real McCoy. *You* did that. His own family didn't know how to do it for him. It wouldn't have happened without you."

Marcus slumped in the bucket seat. It was good to hear it, even if it didn't change anything. Yes, today had been great. But Charlie was still sick . . . and deteriorating. There had never been a case—not one—of somebody with Alzheimer's getting better. No risk, even with the longest odds and the richest payoff, was ever going to make a dent in that.

"I'd better lie low for a while," Marcus mused. "Right now I'm AWOL from the biggest game of the season. Coach is going to cook me on a rotating spit."

Mac chuckled. "Lying low sounds like a good idea. After today you're due for a little downtime."

Suddenly, the squad car emitted three sharp *blurp*s and pulled over to the shoulder. Officer Deluca rolled down the window and indicated with hand signals that the Toyota should do the same.

"What's *this* about?" Marcus wondered aloud.

Deluca jumped out of the patrol car and approached the passenger window. "Jordan!" he ordered. "Get into my car. Hurry."

Marcus was alarmed. "Is something wrong with Charlie?"

"Yeah, Charlie snores. It's annoying. Come on, get in the car." He turned to Mac. "You—obey the speed limit. I'm not going to."

He hustled Marcus out of the Avalon and into the front seat of the cruiser. Then he took off down the road, siren wailing.

"What's going on?" Marcus queried anxiously. "Is it an emergency?"

"Troy Popovich busted up his hand and Calvin Applegate is at quarterback, stinking out the stadium. The second perfect season is on life support."

Marcus stared. "You're taking me to the football game?"

"Barker asked for you by name."

"How did he know where to find me?" Marcus asked, mystified.

"I've been keeping the Popovich family informed on our progress," Deluca explained. "Troy knew you were with me."

Among the strangest parts of a strange day, surely this development was the most bizarre. "Officer Deluca, no offense, but we've been talking about kidnapping, arrest, jail, risking the life of a sick man—but all that's forgotten because the Raiders might *lose*?"

"Cops are practical people, Marcus. Nothing is going to change what happened today. But the game isn't over yet." They swerved around a transport truck. "Sit tight. We'll be there in eight minutes."

Maybe that was why the glaciers had chosen this area to stop their advance, scattering the humongous boulders that Mom loved so well—even though the sport of football would not be developed for tens of thousands of years. On some ancient geological level of awareness, the Ice Age had realized that here, near Kennesaw, it had entered Bizarro World.

Or maybe Officer Deluca's perspective came from the simple fact that, in a small town on a bleak rocky landscape, there was just nothing to think about other than the DNA Raiders.

It definitely took a place like this to produce a Charlie Popovich.

The neighborhoods on the outskirts of Kennesaw were familiar to Marcus now. As the cruiser barreled toward the center of town, cars pulled over to let them through. The police car roared up Poplar Street doing close to seventy. Deluca took the rise so fast that the tires actually left the road surface.

The squad car bounced back to the pavement, jarring Charlie awake. He sat up, groggy and disoriented. "What—?"

He looked around, blinking. They were passing by the towering trees of Three Alarm Park on their left. His bleary eyes finally fixed on the back of Marcus's head. "Mac . . . ?" he began uncertainly.

"Yeah, Charlie, I'm here." Marcus cast a meaningful glance in Deluca's direction. This was not the time for a reality check.

Charlie's gaze swung to the cruiser's opposite flank just in time to catch sight of Kenneth Oliver perched on a step stool, working with pliers to tighten the metal cockroach above the door of his exterminator's shop.

"Like he owns the world," Charlie snorted in disgust. "What do you say we dump out every nail in his store?"

"Next time," Marcus promised in a quiet voice.

All at once, Deluca slammed on the brakes, and the cruiser fishtailed to a halt. "Wait a minute—*he's* the secret accomplice you've been covering for? *Him?*"

Marcus peered very deliberately out the window and said nothing.

"Don't screw around!" the officer persisted. "You're going before a judge for that!"

"Great," Marcus muttered. "So I save my skin, and it gets blamed on a guy with Alzheimer's."

"You can't protect him, Marcus. He's not legally responsible anyway."

Marcus was not consoled. "Then you'll use it as evidence that he's mentally incompetent."

Deluca shook his head sadly. "It's all out in the open now. You taking the rap won't change that."

Marcus blanched. He'd thought he was helping Charlie, but he'd only made everything worse.

Deluca read his mind. "You know, this isn't my first Alzheimer's case. They're usually elderly, but it's the same drill. They wander; they get lost. Even at home, things go wrong. New Paltz P.D. had an eighty-seven-year-old man who tried to microwave a stapler. Burned his whole house down around him. Poor guy survived D-Day, but didn't make it through that. You want your friend to be next?"

Marcus stared stubbornly into the police radio. Deluca was just trying to scare him, but the cop wasn't wrong. If Charlie could try to pay bus fare with a walnut, who knew what else he might be capable of?

Deluca put the car back in gear and off they raced, siren wailing once again. "You're some piece of work, Marcus Jordan—some weird, loyal, stupid piece of work," he said after a moment. "I think I'm starting to like you. I've always been a lousy judge of character."

Marcus shrank back into his seat amid a whirlwind of melancholy thoughts.

Charlie nudged his arm. "What's up with Dr. Demento?" he whispered. "I don't think he's right in the head."

A bitter laugh escaped Marcus. He caught an aggrieved look from Deluca behind the wheel.

"Just relax," he advised Charlie. "We're almost there."

"Where?"

"The football game."

That sounded reasonable to Charlie Popovich. He was going to a football game.

CHAPTER
TWENTY-FOUR

The home stands were quiet at DNA's field, and the scoreboard told the story. With Calvin at quarterback, the Raiders' offense had fizzled, scoring only a single field goal. He had thrown as many interceptions as he had completed passes—two—allowing the Poughkeepsie West Warriors to open up a 14–3 lead. With the game now in the fourth quarter, Kennesaw fans saw their second perfect season circling the drain. To them, the sound of an approaching siren held little interest.

When the squad car screeched to a halt in front of the field house, a mob of parents, students, and groundskeepers swarmed all around. The door was wrenched open, and

Marcus was hauled bodily into the center of this mass of humanity. Helpless to move, he was relieved of his jacket, pants, shirt, and shoes. He could see equipment coming at him, passed from fingertip to fingertip across the top of the crowd, like beach balls at a rock concert. Shoulder pads somehow found their way over his head. A green jersey followed quickly. It wasn't even his stuff, just random gear pillaged from the locker room. Time was ticking away, and not a single snap of potential comeback could be wasted.

"I'll do that!" He snatched the jockstrap out of the hands of somebody's mother and stepped into it a split second before the football pants were run up his legs.

He felt like Pharaoh being dressed by dozens of attendants. The multitude lifted him under the arms and carried him toward the field even as his shoes were being tied. Fully suited up, he was deposited on his feet in front of Coach Barker. A helmet was scrunched down over his ears.

The face on the bobblehead was a thundercloud. "I'd kill you, but it'll have to wait."

All Marcus could think to say was "My shoes are too small."

"You want to play quarterback? Curl your toes." And, propelled by an encouraging slap on the butt, he was in the game.

He got two strides from the sidelines when something cold and hard slammed against his chin protector.

Troy stepped out to block his path. "Where's my dad?"

"He's fine. They're driving him home." Marcus's eyes fell on the ice pack wrapped around the injured quarterback's knuckles. "Wait a minute—shouldn't you be screaming your head off right now?"

"Want me to start?" Troy warned.

"If you've got a broken hand," Marcus insisted, "there's no way can you hit like that and stay standing."

"So now you've graduated medical school?" Troy demanded. "Get in there and do what you have to do! And when it's done, you watch your back, because I'm coming after you!"

"Take a number," Marcus retorted, jogging onto the field.

Ron's was the first face he recognized in the huddle. "Jeez, Marcus, what the hell happened? Where were you?"

"I'm here now. Come on, let's do this."

The drive got off to a shaky start. On first down, Marcus fumbled the snap and was lucky when the center fell back and sat on it. Second down was a wobbly pass that sailed five feet over Luke's head. Facing third and eleven, Marcus fumed his way through a short time-out. He was finally the first-string quarterback of the Raiders, and he was about to get the blame for blowing the second perfect season. Like it was his fault he hadn't taken a single snap in practice for weeks. And all so Barker wouldn't offend the great Troy Popovich, who was on the bench, hiding behind a broken hand . . . that wasn't broken.

Surely that gave Marcus the right to play this *his* way—the way he'd learned from the master. When in doubt, get out there and hit somebody.

The play from the bench was a pass, but Marcus called an audible for a halfback draw. He dropped into the pocket, faked a throw, and slapped the ball into Ron's breadbasket. Then he targeted the biggest monster on the Warriors' line and planted his shoulder so deep into the guy's abdomen that he knocked him back a full five yards. Expecting a pass, the defense was caught flat-footed. By the time they recovered, Ron was through the hole and gone. They managed to haul him down from behind, but by then he had galloped sixty yards. Two plays later, Marcus was in the end zone on a quarterback sneak.

The fans came back to life, and so did Coach Barker, whose head was in full bobble as the crowd roared its approval.

Marcus was so excited that he nearly botched the hold on the extra point. But somehow the kicker managed to get the ball between the uprights, and the Raiders had cut the deficit to 14–10.

On the sidelines Coach Barker greeted his quarterback with an ecstatic bear hug, then held him at arm's length and bawled, "You're not running my plays!"

"It's the shoes." Marcus grinned. "They pinch."

Barker stared at him, perplexed, but he asked no

questions. He did not want to argue with the sole ray of sunshine on this dark day.

As Marcus took the field to play cornerback on defense, Alyssa grasped his arm as he passed her. "One more score, Marcus! I know you can do it!"

He inclined his head toward Troy on the bench. "What happened to him?"

"Can't really tell." She turned uncharacteristically serious. "I'm kind of worried about him."

And before he could reply, a whistle called him into formation.

The Raiders' defense held firm, and four plays later, Marcus was back under center, armed with another Barker play that he didn't intend to execute. No football team had anything in the playbook that made a hard-hitting blocker out of the quarterback. But that's exactly what Marcus was now—taking on much larger opponents, running right over them, and then looking for someone else to flatten. The Raiders' offense ground out yardage with old-school smashmouth football, gaining five or six yards at a try, piling up first downs. Then, just when the Warriors had settled in to defend the running attack, Marcus uncorked a long pass to Calvin, who had snuck unobserved into the end zone: 17–14, Raiders. The crowd went berserk.

Tasting victory, the defense returned to protect its three-point lead for the final four minutes. *One more stop should do it,* Marcus thought, lining up at cornerback. Then they could play possession and eat up the clock.

Running out of time, the visitors grew desperate, launching hurried passes their receivers had little chance of catching. Soon it was fourth and ten, and the Warriors' offense had no choice but to try a Hail Mary. The long throw was tipped at the line of scrimmage, and it twirled in a lofty arc—a high-flying bean in the late-afternoon sky, anybody's ball.

Marcus was determined to get there first. He was airborne, diving for the spot where it would come down. He registered the touch of his fingertips on the pigskin, the texture of the laces as he began to gather it in.

He was so focused on making the catch that he never saw the offensive lineman, even though the kid must have weighed nearly three hundred pounds. He was running full out when his knee slammed into Marcus's helmet. The impact was like being hit by a small car.

Marcus heard rather than felt the collision and was aware of a violent motion deep inside his skull.

Pop!

Darkness.

CHAPTER
TWENTY-FIVE

The kiss was soft and—skillful?

Marcus had no idea where he was, but as he rose through hazy semiconsciousness, he knew the unmistakable silky pressure of lips against his own.

Am I dreaming?

It felt like a dream—those last few seconds before waking.

But whose lips—?

Troy grabbed Alyssa by the back of the cheerleading tunic and yanked her off Marcus's prostrate form. *"Jeez, Lyss—"*

She cut him off. "He's waking up!"

Marcus's eyelids fluttered.

Dr. Prossky held a tiny bottle of smelling salts under the injured player's nose. Marcus's head jerked as he tried to avoid the powerful odor, and he sat up in the coach's arms.

"Easy, kid," Barker ordered. "You're okay."

Marcus took in the stadium, the crowd noise, the circle of anxious faces around him.

The coach answered his unasked question. "You got kneed in the coconut by a bull moose."

Dr. Prossky shone a penlight into Marcus's eyes. "Pupils are responding." He held up a V-for-victory sign. "How many fingers?"

Marcus's returning focus shifted from the doctor's hand to the scoreboard. "Three."

"Three?" bawled the coach.

Marcus struggled to his feet. "Three-point game." He picked up his helmet and crammed it down over his head.

The rush was sudden and violent, like an explosion inside his skull. For one frantic moment, he was afraid he might leave his lunch on the turf in front of him. The nausea passed, but the tight headgear caused a persistent ringing in his ears.

Barker gazed anxiously into his quarterback's eyes. "You're good to go, right?"

"I'm fine," Marcus replied firmly, figuring if he said it enough, that would make it so. And he felt fine—sort of. Except for that rice pudding where his knees used to be. Jogging in place made that go away, but it amped up the ringing, so he could hardly hear it when the doctor pronounced him fit to return to the game.

Everyone looked to the unofficial member of the Raiders' coaching staff—the head cheerleader.

Alyssa shrugged. "It's a contact sport. You can't take out every guy who gets his bell rung. Otherwise there'd be nobody left on the field."

"I agree," put in Dr. Prossky. "This isn't uncommon."

Barker put his arm around Marcus's shoulders. "Okay, kid, this is almost over. Just get in there and hand off quick. The guys will protect you. And for God's sake, no more of that blocking. Okay, go."

"Don't," came a quiet voice behind them.

Troy.

The coach frowned mightily. "Stay out of this, Popovich. Who asked you?"

"Don't do it, man," Troy told Marcus. "I'll take the snaps."

"What about your broken hand?" the coach demanded.

"I said I'll take the snaps."

Marcus regarded him in suspicion. "This is my game. Let me finish it."

"Don't," Troy repeated softly. "You don't want to end up like him."

"End up like *who*?" the coach bawled. "What are you talking about?"

Marcus bit back an angry comeback. Even in his muzzy state, he couldn't help but notice what was different about this conversation. Troy *never* brought up the subject of his father and the illness that was slowly destroying him. This was as good as a lie detector test. He was trying to do the right thing—for someone he obviously loathed. It was as heroic as anything he had ever accomplished on a football field.

Marcus pulled off his helmet, struggling to tune out the ringing. "Maybe I *am* a little dizzy," he admitted, and took a seat on the bench.

Barker was close to hysterics. "*Somebody* get in there!"

Troy began to unwrap the tape around his ice pack.

CHAPTER
TWENTY-SIX

Troy Popovich ran seven plays for a total of twenty-four yards and two first downs. It was a remarkably unheroic drive in an otherwise stellar high school career, but it was enough to kill the clock and win the game for the Raiders.

It was also the last time Number Seven would ever play football.

At practice on Monday, he simply was not there. Coach Barker communicated the news to his stunned team with his usual deadpan delivery. Troy was out; Marcus was in. "Drop and give me twenty push-ups."

If Troy had told the coach the reason for his sudden retirement, Barker was opting to guard the privacy of the quarterback who had brought so much success to DNA football.

"Does he really have a broken hand?" Ron probed.

"He has *none of your business*, Rorschach!" Barker snapped. "Here's what this means to you. Popovich used to be QB. Now it's Jordan. Got it? It's not rocket science."

The final hurdle in the way of Marcus's ascension to the starting job was cleared after practice in the office of Kennesaw's general practitioner.

"I see no ill effects whatsoever," proclaimed Dr. Antilla. "If there was brain trauma, it must have been very slight."

"I sat out for nothing," Marcus said.

The doctor shook his head. "There's an odd math to concussions. One plus one doesn't equal two. When they're close together, one plus one equals fifty. Some sports researchers have begun to draw connections between frequent concussions and neurological disorders like Parkinson's and Alzheimer's."

"I think I heard something about that," Marcus mumbled unhappily.

And now Mom had heard about it, too, which meant the cat was out of the bag. "Marcus, I don't know about this anymore. Are you sure you're safe?"

"Is anybody?" he challenged her.

"I don't care about anybody. I only care about you. It's pretty obvious that Troy Popovich got so spooked that he had to quit."

"We can't know for sure what Troy was thinking," Marcus reminded her. "We don't read minds, and even if we did, Troy's wouldn't be my choice of reading material."

"Well, how would *you* explain it?" she persisted. "I'm told Troy was the best ever around here. What else would make him give it up?"

The best ever. *Even from my own mother.*

"Maybe that's the whole point, Mom. Troy *wasn't* the best because he *could* give it up. He was good, but there was something missing—the desire, the passion for the game. He just didn't . . ."

His voice trailed off. He'd almost finished with *He just didn't love the pop,* but that probably wasn't the best thing for Barbara Jordan to hear right then. Still, tragedy affected people in different ways, and it made sense that it would affect Charlie's son most of all. Troy had to hang up his cleats; Marcus couldn't wait to get back in there and cream somebody. To him, that was the ultimate tribute to the King of Pop.

Aloud, he said, "I promise I'll be safe. I'll know when it's time to get off the field."

But *would* he know? On Saturday, he'd been all gung ho to finish the game. Jerk or not, he'd always owe Troy for keeping him on the sidelines.

Mrs. Jordan's interest in Charlie's condition wasn't just a campaign to scare Marcus off football. Mom was so genuinely relieved to learn from Officer Deluca that her son wasn't a juvenile delinquent—that Marcus's mystery accomplice actually existed—that she was blabbing it to everybody who would listen.

"Jeez, Mom, respect the guy's privacy!" Marcus exploded. "How would you like your private family business advertised on a Times Square billboard?"

"Well, I have to tell your father," she reasoned. "We need to quash whatever ideas he might have gotten about having me declared an unfit parent."

"Fine, but only Stalin. And maybe his lawyer."

"And my boss at the paper," she added. "He sees the police blotter, Marcus! Humor me, will you? I'm so happy you're not in trouble anymore. According to Michael—"

"Michael?"

"Officer Deluca. He said the fact that you were just covering for Charlie changes everything about your case."

That was a positive development. But . . . Michael?

The plot thickened on Tuesday, when Marcus returned from practice to find Officer Deluca ensconced at the kitchen table.

"Great—you're home," said Mrs. Jordan. "Tell him, Michael."

"The December second court date has been canceled—all charges dropped," Deluca announced. "You're clean, Marcus."

He was grateful to be off the hook for Charlie's antics against Kenneth Oliver, but why hadn't the officer delivered the news by phone? The only thing worse than trouble with the cops was having Mike Deluca hitting on your mother.

Maybe he was reading too much into it. On the other hand, Mom deserved to be happy. Seventeen years of marriage to Comrade Stalin—if there was ever a definition of "suffered enough," that had to be it. Now she had freedom, the Gunks, and a nonfelon for a son. Barbara Jordan had finally hit the trifecta. Good for her.

But he drew the line at Mom telling her editor the real reason behind Marcus's legal problems. "Let him think I'm an ax murderer for all I care. You can't tell a small-town paper that its most famous citizen has Alzheimer's."

He owed that much to Charlie.

Marcus looked at Three Alarm Park as if he'd never seen it before in his life. How much had the world changed since he and Charlie had first played football here? Part of him was waiting for the NFL veteran to burst out of the bushes and unleash one of the famous pops that had earned him his nickname.

No. That hint of movement atop the Paper Airplane? Just a squirrel. Anyway, he should know better than to look for Charlie. It wasn't likely that the family would let him wander around on his own again. Marcus had himself to thank for that.

Yet the sculpture called to him—almost as if, by climbing to the King of Pop's aerie, he would somehow be closer to the man himself. He began to ascend one of the smooth granite flukes, amazed that he felt absolutely no fear of falling. Here was the payoff from all those weeks of Camp Popovich: His center of gravity was low, his balance as steady as the heavy stone he was standing on. He had never understood the former linebacker's attraction to perilous perches until this moment. To Charlie, they weren't perilous at all.

He sat at the top and enjoyed a Charlie's-eye view of the park. This must have been one of the few experiences that still made total sense to Charlie—something he could remember from the past *and* experience in the present. Marcus stayed up there, drinking it in, for more than an hour before the cold wind drove him down.

Back on the Vespa, on Poplar Street, he suddenly found himself face-to-fang with Kenneth Oliver. The exterminator didn't exactly look happy to see him, but the warlike animosity seemed to be absent. And could that be a little embarrassment softening the man's perpetual outrage?

"Officer Deluca explained the misunderstanding."

Marcus nodded curtly. Still, he vowed to himself that one insult, one derogatory word against Charlie, and Deluca was going to have to set another court date—this one for assault.

But the exterminator had no interest in reassigning blame. Instead, he said, "I have something for you."

He stepped into his shop and emerged a moment later holding an old photograph in a cracked frame.

Marcus accepted it with a frown.

"It was in the basement of my store," Mr. Oliver explained. "I didn't realize what it was until Officer Deluca came to explain about Mr. Popovich."

Marcus examined the picture. It featured a proprietor standing in the doorway of K.O. Pest Control, minus the giant cockroach. The sign in the window—DINGLEY'S HARDWARE EMPORIUM—matched the one in the print outside Mom's office at the newspaper. From the sour expression on Old Man Dingley's face, Marcus could tell he was twice the stinker Kenneth Oliver was on his worst day. No wonder Charlie mixed the two up. They were practically brothers across time. This was, without question, a guy who deserved to have every nail in his store dumped out and mixed up.

"Why give it to me?" Marcus asked.

And then he saw why. Reflected in the plate glass below the lettering were two kids—boys, probably about twelve or thirteen. While it was impossible to tell from a simple still shot that they were up to no good, Marcus could see that this was a pair of natural hell-raisers. One of them had dark, unruly curls.

Charlie. Marcus would have bet his life on it. The other boy was indistinct, his face half hidden beneath the visor of a baseball cap. But it was a pretty good bet that this was Charlie's partner in crime, James McTavish.

"I thought you might know someone who'd want this," the exterminator explained.

Was that a smile? Not possible.

"Thanks," he said. "I'll see that he gets it."

Marcus stood on the porch of the Popovich home, the Dingley picture under his arm, feeling foolish. How could he possibly be welcome in this place after EBU homecoming? After *everything*?

He might never have worked up the courage to ring the bell if Chelsea hadn't noticed him there and opened the door. "You."

"Hi. Uh—where's Troy?"

She was annoyed. "Do I look like his secretary? He's got a life again, since quitting football. You should try it sometime."

Marcus shuffled uncomfortably. "I'd better go. I just came here to bring you this."

Her eyes fell on the picture in Marcus's hands. "What is it?"

He held out the broken frame. "Check out the kids reflected in the window. Isn't that your dad on the left?"

She examined the image. "Maybe. I'll show Mom." She frowned. "Where'd you get it?"

"It's kind of a long story." Marcus hesitated. "How's Charlie doing? Is he okay?"

He saw a brief flash of anger in her eyes, but it passed quickly. She seemed to be weighing his interest, deciding if it was genuine—or even whether or not he had the right to be interested.

"I'm not sure," she replied at last. "I don't trust myself anymore. When I thought I knew how he was, he turned out to be much worse."

Marcus hung his head. "Thanks to me."

"No," she said gently. "Taking Dad to homecoming was the right thing to do. *We* should have done it. Mom thinks so. Even Troy thinks so now."

Marcus, however, felt that he might never be sure. The moment of triumph had been so fleeting compared with the grim reality of what was in store for Charlie.

Chelsea hugged the picture. "Listen, I'm glad you're here."

He managed a crooked smile. "No, you're not."

"My mom was going to call. We need some help with Daddy, and we know he really responds to you. It's okay if you want to say no."

The Kennesaw Retirement Lodge resembled a gracious old manor house nestled among rolling hills and rich greenery. The elegant lobby could have been the reception area in any five-star resort in the country. But underneath the scent of fresh flowers and furniture polish, Marcus detected the antiseptic smell of a hospital—a harsh reminder of what this place truly was.

"I appreciate your coming with us today," Mrs. Popovich murmured to Marcus. "Charlie really likes you, even if he thinks you're someone else."

"I'm happy to help," Marcus stammered. In actuality,

he would have traded all that he owned to be anywhere else. But he owed this family. It was the least he could do.

What a procession they made. Chelsea and her mother, devastated; Troy, tight-lipped, trapped between anger and sorrow; Marcus, uncomfortable and out of place. Only Charlie seemed untouched by the crushing weight of where they were and what their business was.

"I've never seen so many old people in my life. What is this, the Crypt Keeper family reunion?"

Such a comment normally would have triggered at least a snicker from Marcus, but nothing seemed funny right now. Charlie's observation had a deeper truth behind it. The lodge's residents *were* old. The youngest of them must have had twenty years on Charlie. Many seemed to be in their nineties or even older. Not all were in ill health, but there were a lot of canes, walkers, and wheelchairs. It was hard to picture an NFL linebacker, not far from peak physical condition, living here.

Troy was thinking the same thing. "This was a mistake," he said grimly. "We're leaving."

Mrs. Molloy, the social worker who was serving as their guide, smiled understandingly. "I know it can be jarring at first—"

Troy cut her off. "My father doesn't belong here."

The social worker was patient. "We're the facility that's equipped and staffed to deal with his particular problem. It just so happens that most people with the same special needs are considerably older."

In a small lounge at the end of the hall, three wheelchair-bound ladies sat staring at a television set that exhibited nothing but snow. Their concentration was intense and unwavering.

It was sad, and Charlie must have thought so, too, because he walked over, picked up the remote, and changed the channel for them. "Better, right?"

He got no response. No one even blinked. If the viewers noticed that the show they were now watching was any different from the nothing that had preceded it, they gave no indication.

Charlie sat down in an empty chair and began to watch with them. In an instant, his expression was as blank as theirs. He blended in perfectly, as if he had always been there.

Mrs. Molloy nodded approvingly. "You see? He'll be helpful to the older residents while receiving the services he needs."

"Wait a minute." Charlie was suddenly on his feet again, facing them accusingly. "You're talking about *me*? Living *here*?"

Mrs. Popovich rushed to her husband and took his hand. "Charlie," she began huskily. "You don't understand—"

"Do you think I'm blind?" he bellowed. "I know what this place is! It's an old folks' home, and it has nothing to do with me! Okay, sure, maybe I forget a few things but—" He stopped short, looking anxiously from face to face—his wife, his daughter, his son, and finally Marcus.

He frowned uncertainly. "Mac?" It was almost a plea. If this truly was his old friend Mac, then that was proof that his concept of the universe still made sense.

Marcus was struck dumb. This was the first time Charlie had ever called him Mac outside the context of football. He hesitated. It would have been easy to say yes, just as he had dozens of times before. He'd become so accustomed to playing the role of Mac that he'd actually caught himself thinking as if he *were* Mac.

But now, in this place, he could not bring himself to perpetuate the lie. It would offer the King of Pop a few seconds of comfort while putting off what genuinely needed to happen for the man's own welfare and safety. Would that be doing Charlie a favor?

He looked desperately to Mrs. Popovich for some kind of guidance. Yes, he was here for support, but this was too much to put on his shoulders! He knew in an instant that there would be no help from Charlie's wife. Her eyes were so filled with tears that he doubted she could even see him.

He shook his head sadly. "My name is Marcus Jordan."

Twin streaks coursed down the former linebacker's flushed cheeks. A muffled sob escaped Chelsea; Troy turned away. Mrs. Popovich took her husband's arm and held on, as if she could keep him with her simply by not letting him go. Marcus was turned to stone at the sight of this NFL veteran—husband, father, tower of strength—weeping like a frightened child.

Before this moment, the very nature of Charlie's confusion had protected him from the truth of his situation. But at last, he was face-to-face with the fact that his life was never going to be the same again.

CHAPTER
TWENTY-SEVEN

It was the perfect early-December day for the last football game of the year. The temperature hovered around fifty, mostly because of the bright sunshine pouring out of a clear blue sky.

The DNA bleachers were packed and boisterous. Virtually all of Kennesaw was there to see history made with the completion of a second perfect season. The Raiders and their first-string quarterback, Marcus Jordan, were already up to a two-touchdown lead against their hapless opponents, the three-and-six Latham Lions.

The next play was a quick pitch, followed by a teeth-jarring block to spring Ron for a twelve-yard gain. It wasn't typical quarterback play—from midget leagues to the pros, coaches pampered their precious field generals. Marcus was pretty sure that half the time he did it just to watch Barker squirm.

And because he loved the pop. He'd learned that from the King himself.

He drank in the crowd noise, the chorus of cheerleaders chanting his name. In a way, this would always be Troy's team, but the guys—and the town—had made a place for Marcus, too. Especially since Number Seven's new position was in the bleachers next to his father. Mrs. Popovich had lost interest in the Raiders the minute Troy was sidelined, and Chelsea's football boycott was still in full force. That left the ex–Golden Boy to accompany Charlie to watch the sport he still loved and had once played better than all but a few. It had to hurt for Troy to watch Marcus in his old job, but there he was, even cheering a little. Troy Popovich was a major jerk, but this was pretty damn loyal. You had to give him that.

At the thought of Charlie, Marcus bobbled a snap and had to fall on the ball at the bottom of a pile of Lions.

"Head in the game, Jordan!" bawled Barker from the bench.

The images of last month's visit to the Kennesaw Retirement Lodge had become a haunting screen saver in Marcus's brain, popping up whenever he wasn't actively thinking about something else. It had to be fifty times worse for Charlie's family. And Charlie himself? In all likelihood, the former linebacker had forgotten the facility and the fact that his name was now on the waiting list for the next available room there. Still, there was something different about him. According to Chelsea, his energy level was down and he was acting withdrawn. And while that may have been common for a man Charlie's age, it wasn't the norm for this NFL veteran, perhaps the world's oldest juvenile delinquent.

"It's like he suddenly got old," she had told Marcus. "Maybe he doesn't remember the visit, but he senses something's up. Something sad."

Marcus slapped his own helmet, willing himself to concentrate. It was almost halftime. Soon the season would be over, and he would own a piece of the glory that Troy had tried so hard to keep from him.

He flattened a two-hundred-sixty-pound nose tackle, and Ron rambled through the gap, penetrating to the Latham twenty-seven-yard line. The crowd came back to life. Another touchdown, and a 21–0 lead, would seal the game. The bleachers seemed to undulate as the spectators got to their feet, exhorting the offense to put this one away.

Barker must have felt the same way. The next call amounted to a knockout punch—a play-action pass to the end zone.

Marcus faked a handoff and rolled right, scanning for his receiver. Luke had a step on his man and was galloping down the sidelines. It was all in the timing. The throw had to hit Luke in stride, past the defender. Delicate, but doable.

Marcus measured the distance, cocked back his arm . . . and froze. At the edge of his field of vision, he caught sight of a familiar figure, tall and broad, taking the stadium stairs three at a time. *Charlie?* His eyes sought out Troy, who was absorbed in the drama on the field. Troy could've made this pass easily and probably wanted to see if Marcus could do the same.

He's probably hoping I miss!

Whatever the reason, the guy didn't notice that his father had left his side.

Out of time, Marcus pulled the ball down and sidestepped a charging linebacker.

His teammates were screaming at him, practically with one voice: *"Throw!"*

Luke was all alone in the end zone, waving wildly.

But Marcus's gaze moved inexorably back to Charlie. Why was he climbing the bleachers with such singleness of purpose?

And then Marcus saw it.

Perched on the iron railing that ran around the rim of the stadium was a large gray-brown hawk. The voice of James McTavish came to him: *I never once set foot on that field without looking up to the back of the bleachers, half expecting to see Harry finally making his way home. . . .*

Could Charlie be reliving *that*? Did he believe the hawk up there was Harry, the mascot he'd birdnapped and set free all those years ago? The picture Mac had painted was vivid: Charlie tightrope walking on the ledge of the stadium four stories up.

"Troy!" he bellowed. But there was no chance of reaching him over the roar of the crowd.

"Throw it, Jordan!" howled Barker, his bobblehead threatening to blast off his body.

Marcus tucked the ball into the crook of his arm and headed for the stands. He blew by his apoplectic coach, dropped the ball at the man's feet, and hit the stairs at a full sprint.

The crowd's roar of agony soon turned to bewilderment. Surely this had never happened before in all of football history. Why would a quarterback run not merely out-of-bounds but off the field and clear up the bleachers?

For the first time, Troy noticed his father's absence and looked around in alarm. Charlie had almost reached the top when Troy spotted him. He was barreling along the last row, heading for the place where the hawk perched majestically, settling its feathers.

Never, under any circumstances, could Marcus recall a higher level of performance intensity than during his charge up those stairs. "Charlie!" It was barely a rasp. One hundred percent of his effort was channeled into pure speed.

Charlie was just a few feet away from the hawk, and he must have felt it was time to make his move. With the agility of the high school boy he sometimes thought he was, he climbed up onto the concrete lip of the stadium, the rail mere inches above his ankles.

Marcus heard Troy shouting, but he was too focused on the senior Popovich to turn back toward him. Charlie was twenty feet away, shuffling along the parapet toward the bird.

Marcus allowed himself the tiniest breath, the most minuscule hesitation, in order to shout, *"Stop!"*

And Charlie did stop, poised on the rim, perfectly balanced. He turned and fixed Marcus with a penetrating stare.

Marcus was turned to stone. He had seen the King of Pop look this way only once before—on the podium at EBU homecoming, during his induction into the university's hall of fame.

He took another step and reached for the bird. Marcus closed his eyes in silent prayer, just for an instant. And when he opened them again, Charlie Popovich was gone.

CHAPTER
TWENTY-EIGHT

Marcus hadn't been to a funeral since he was eight. Great-grandpa Benjamin, from the Stalin side of the family, whose birth predated the *Titanic*, had died at the ripe old age of ninety-nine. The service had been low-key, attended by just a handful of family members.

"Where is everybody?" Marcus remembered asking his mother.

She had gestured around the cemetery. "They're already here."

Great-grandpa had lived long enough to bury just about everybody he'd ever known. But that had left virtually no one to pay their last respects when his turn finally came around.

The opposite was true for Charlie. At only fifty-four, he was among the first of his peer group to die, so hordes of mourners packed the chapel. By the time Marcus and his mother got there, the seating area was already full. They huddled under a too-small umbrella in the parking lot with countless other latecomers, listening to the eulogy as it was amplified on an external speaker. A fine mist rendered uncomfortable clothing even more so, but a damp suit was the last thing on Marcus's mind.

Most of Kennesaw was there. Apparently, there were no hard feelings against Charlie for putting a permanent asterisk beside the Raiders' back-to-back perfect seasons. Now the final game would never be completed, due to the tragedy in the stadium.

Standing there in the rain, it struck Marcus that when all was said and done, the Popovich family had succeeded in keeping Charlie's disease a secret. Despite the attention he had received as the town hero, only Marcus had figured out that the man had been suffering from Alzheimer's. In a way, the former linebacker's celebrity had shielded him from real scrutiny—he was "charismatic," "quirky," "a real local character." Marcus alone had been close enough to see deeper—just as Marcus had been the closest at the very end.

To him, it still played like a clip of sadistic film editing—Charlie on the ledge . . . quick cut . . . the ledge and no Charlie.

It was the last thing he remembered in sharp focus that day. The rest had been filtered through a lens of tears. The multicolored blur of the agitated crowd; someone who might have been Troy running past him on the bleachers. In the confusion, everybody was charging *up* the stands, while Marcus was charging *down*. At that point, only he knew that the scene of the accident was no longer at the top of the stadium but on the pavement four stories below. And when he burst through the exit—

Marcus had seen firsthand the ravages of memory loss. But some memories were best forgotten.

In addition to the Kennesaw people, there were also quite a few NFL veterans who had made the trip to Charlie's funeral. Marcus couldn't put names to the faces, but there was no mistaking the football players. Even now, many years into retirement, they looked like mountains wearing suits. Their thick necks bulged within tight, starched collars.

After the graveside service, the crowd began to thin out. Only relatives and close friends returned to the Popovich house in support of the bereaved family.

Mrs. Jordan pulled up to the curb at the end of the long front walk.

"Are you sure you want to go in?" she asked her son.

He sighed. "I'm sure I *don't* want to go in. But I'm going anyway."

She ruffled his hair. "You're a really good kid, Marcus.

And I hope you'll forgive me for thinking that maybe you weren't."

Marcus nodded gravely. "Understandable. When Officer Mike is on the trail of a serial toilet paperer—"

She skewered him with a sharp look. "What is it with you and him?"

He shrugged. "Nothing. I've got no hard feelings. He's a pretty good guy. . . ." He gave her a meaningful look.

Her eyes narrowed. "What?"

"I don't know. Seems like you two are getting pretty friendly."

"A word of advice," she said. "Back off. You're my son, not my life coach." But as she drove away, he could see she was smiling a little.

Entering the Popovich house, Marcus had been expecting the worst. Instead, the place resembled a crowded short-order restaurant, with a constant supply of drinks and sandwiches being paraded from the kitchen.

The buzz of conversation was about Charlie, but other topics too—the weather, politics, and, inevitably, football. Old friends and family reminisced, and the memories were fond and happy ones.

Marcus spotted Troy at the center of a group of Raiders, all of them fidgeting in their jackets and ties. Alyssa was by Troy's side, hanging off his arm, in fact—closer than close. Marcus had noticed them at the cemetery, too, but under the circumstances, he hadn't really given it much thought. Now he could see that the on-again, off-again relationship was definitely on again. More than that, she was a full mourner, stunning in black—a bona fide member of the family. That was going to gag Chelsea—then again, the poor girl probably had other things on her mind today.

Alyssa's eyes met his, and Marcus quickly turned away, focusing his attention on a tray of sandwiches on a nearby table. He picked up an egg salad triangle and nibbled a tiny bite from the corner, not because he was hungry, but because even now—even *here*—Alyssa had the power to unsettle him. He'd given up on her and didn't even care very much, but for some reason it stung that she was back with Troy.

He stared into the platter until the cellophane decorations on the toothpicks blurred into a kaleidoscope. A moment later, there was a light touch on his elbow, and he heard Alyssa's voice.

"I wanted to explain. You know, before you saw me and Troy together."

Marcus's tiny bite went down like a bowling ball. "You don't owe me any explanation."

"Troy needs me," she forged on. "I see that now. He only pushed me away because he didn't want anybody to find out what was happening to his dad."

So she knew about that, too. *Troy must be pretty serious this time.* That secret was for family only—if you didn't count the young intruder who had stuck his nose where it wasn't wanted.

"And you need Troy," he told her. "You *always* needed Troy. Even when it was about me, it was about him."

She flushed. "I guess it seems like I'm a total bitch who was only using you to get at Troy. But when it was going on, you and me, I was—into it."

Marcus nodded. "Same here."

He felt stupid, because given half a chance, what guy wouldn't be "into it" with Alyssa Fontaine? But he took her at her word when she said she hadn't meant to mess with his head. She wasn't a malicious person. Besides, he'd always have her football heart. Troy may have been the man of her romantic dreams, but when her fantasies drifted to blocking schemes and power sweeps, the guy with his hands by the center's butt would be Marcus Jordan.

The rain had finally stopped, and some of the NFL players were gathered on the patio, swapping Charlie stories, arguing good-naturedly about which one of them the King of Pop had hit the hardest.

"I heard bells for a week. . . ."

"Remember my torn ACL? That was courtesy of Guess Who. . . ."

"My head went one way, my body the other. . . ."

As Charlie's earliest tackling dummy, James McTavish was right in the middle of it, telling the tale of Harry the Hawk. "I think that's why he went up there in the first place," Charlie's oldest friend was saying. "He was back in that moment at the top of the stadium with Harry. And then—I don't know—he must have just put a foot wrong, and that was all it took."

Marcus had a flashback—Charlie, dancing along the top rail, seconds before his fall. That last look Charlie had cast at Marcus—the King of Pop hadn't been caught up in any moment from the past. He hadn't seemed confused or impaired. His eyes had been clear and lucid and knowing.

"Marcus!" Mac spotted him standing there by the screen door. "This is the kid I was telling you about."

Marcus shook beefy hands all the way around the circle, hearing names he knew from NFL history. This should have been a big moment for a high school football player. But all he could think of was escape.

He stammered his excuses and rushed back into the house, as if removing himself from Mac's presence could wipe the images of that day from his mind. He'd find a phone, call Mom for a lift, get away from here.

He was moving so fast that he nearly collided with Chelsea in the kitchen. This was the first time he'd talked with her since her father's death, and the emotion just poured out of him.

"I never should have stuck myself into your family's business, or pretended to be someone I wasn't! I'm so sorry—"

Suddenly, her arms were around him, cutting off the torrent of apology and self-doubt. Chelsea, who had just come from burying her father, was offering comfort and support to the outsider who had invaded all their lives.

"You were great for Daddy," she whispered. "And he loved you."

It was no consolation. Words—even those words—would never undo what had happened.

"I—I should get going," he said finally.

She nodded. "Thanks for coming." Then she paused. "See you at school."

"Definitely." Marcus was surprised to find himself looking forward to that moment.

He decided to walk home, even though it was a few miles in iffy weather. He needed to clear his head. Charlie's death had seemed so huge, it was easy to forget that the sun was going to rise tomorrow. Marcus would go to school, resume his life, find something to do now that football season was over. Maybe he'd even join Mom on one of her shooting trips into the Gunks. She deserved a little family time that didn't incur lawyer's fees.

He was about to let himself out the door when he heard the sound of a TV coming from a small study off the front hall. It wasn't very loud, but there was no mistaking the roar of a sports crowd and the excited chatter of a color commentator.

Who watches a football game at a funeral reception?

Curious, he poked his head in the doorway. The blinds were drawn, and the light from the monitor danced across the face of the room's lone occupant.

Troy.

Quickly, he tried to retreat, but Troy had already seen him and was waving him inside.

All right, Marcus thought with resignation. *Only because he's Charlie's son. If it'll ease his grief today of all days to punch me out, then it's a small price to pay.*

He entered cautiously. "You know how sorry I am about your dad."

Troy gestured to the TV. "Take a look at this."

Marcus walked over and examined the screen. It was a football game all right, although the picture quality was poor, the uniforms were unfamiliar, the helmets smaller and shaped wrong somehow.

Then he realized that this was the NFL, but from nearly three decades ago—the Bengals against the 49ers.

". . . There's the handoff to Craig . . . whoa! Hammered by Popovich for a loss! No wonder they call him the King of Pop! What a wallop! . . ."

Mesmerized by the action on the screen, Marcus sat down beside Troy, and the two took in the rest of the Bengals' defensive series.

Number 55 was all over the field, his energy boundless, his desire for contact evident. His performance wouldn't have appeared on any highlight reel by today's standards—he made no sack, forced no fumble, created no interception. But he could be seen on every tackle, an arm wrapped around the ballcarrier's ankle, a hand slapping at the pigskin, even a fistful of jersey, slowing up the runner so a teammate could make the stop. He was the kind of blue-collar player who never got the glory yet without whom no team could be successful.

"He was amazing," Marcus said reverently.

"Amazing," Troy agreed soberly. "I've been watching these old films ever since he got sick. And all I can think of is which hit was the one that did it to him? Was it the helmet-to-helmet in Cleveland? The punt-return cover in the Meadowlands? One of his six concussions? And how many concussions were there that he didn't admit to? Where he climbed right back into the meat grinder because 'you've got to be tough to play in this league'?"

I love the pop. . . . Charlie's own words echoed in Marcus's head as he watched number 55 get up from another collision. The poor guy on the screen had no idea that the very same pop that had become his trademark was also silently planting the seeds of his destruction.

Aloud, Marcus said, "I never thanked you for keeping me out of the Poughkeepsie West game."

"I never thanked you for taking my dad to EBU."

Marcus had entered the study anticipating a punch in the face or worse. Instead, he left with his first-ever handshake from Charlie's son.

The weather improved during the walk home. By the time he reached Three Alarm Park, the sun was peeking out from behind the clouds, and the rain seemed to be gone for good.

The park was deserted, just as it had been only three months ago when new arrival Marcus Jordan's solo football practice had been crashed by a mysterious middle-aged man. It felt like a lifetime, and in a way it was—the rest of Charlie's life.

Across Poplar Street, the big metal cockroach loomed above the entrance to K.O. Pest Control. Marcus fought off an irrational compulsion to buy a bag of sugar and pour it in through the mail slot.

A tribute to absent friends.

GORDON KORMAN has written more than fifty middle-grade and teen novels. Favorites include the *New York Times* #1 bestseller *The 39 Clues: One False Note, The Juvie Three, Son of the Mob, Born to Rock,* and *Schooled.* Though he didn't play football in high school, Gordon's been a lifelong fan and season ticket holder. He says, "I've always been fascinated by the 'culture of collision' in football and wanted to explore it—not just from the highlight films but from its darker side as well."

Gordon lives with his family on Long Island, New York. You can visit him online at www.gordonkorman.com.